"This is where we
say goodbye, Kate."

Sean held out his hand to her,
changing with that one gesture from
the husband and lover of the past
twenty-four hours into a polite
stranger.

"When will I see you again?" she asked
desperately. "Will you write?"

"I'm not promising anything." He
stared at her, a frown darkening his
eyes. "It would be best if you do as I
suggested about our marriage," he
added quietly. "Take care, Kate."

"You, too," she whispered as he turned
and walked away.

Blinded by sudden tears, Kate fought
back a great urge to run after him and
beg him not to leave her. Her San
Marco adventure was over, was
already becoming a memory. And the
future, vague and shadowy, was
beginning to claim her....

FLORA KIDD
is also the author of these

Harlequin Presents

and these

Harlequin Romances

Many of these titles are available at your local bookseller.

For a free catalogue listing all available Harlequin Romances
and Harlequin Presents, send your name and address to:

HARLEQUIN READER SERVICE,
M.P.O. Box 707, Niagara Falls, NY 14302
Canadian address: Stratford, Ontario N5A 6W2

FLORA KIDD

beyond control

Harlequin Books

TORONTO • LONDON • LOS ANGELES • AMSTERDAM
SYDNEY • HAMBURG • PARIS • STOCKHOLM • ATHENS • TOKYO

Harlequin Presents edition published June 1981
ISBN 0-373-10434-0

Original hardcover edition published in 1981
by Mills & Boon Limited.

CHAPTER ONE

IN one of the small cell-like rooms of the Santa Rosa Mission a young woman of about twenty-one years of age sat on the edge of the narrow bed and stared blankly at the motes of dust, which were floating in the shaft of yellow sunlight slanting in through the narrow barred window. She was dressed in a cheap white cotton T-shirt and a plain grey cotton skirt which was gathered on elastic at the waist. Her oval face would have been pretty if it had not been so thin and pale. From her high forehead her hair, a dingy reddish-brown in colour, was drawn back and tied with a piece of string at the nape of her neck. Her whole attitude as she sat slumped on the bed was one of forlorn apathy.

A knock sounded on the solid wooden door of the room. She turned her head towards the door slowly as if the movement hurt her.

'Come in.' She spoke listlessly. The day was already hot and she would be glad when *siesta* time came. Then the shutters would close out the sunshine and she would be able to lie down on the bed. To sleep? She doubted it. She had slept very little during the past few days and nights, disturbed like everyone else in the Mission by the sound of gun fire and bomb explosions coming from the city.

The door swung open and a small plump woman dressed in the grey gown and white coif worn by the nuns of the Mission entered. Her perfect white teeth flashed against the smooth golden tan of her face as she smiled.

'A friend of yours has come to see you at last,' she announced in heavily accented English. 'A young man.'

'From England?' The young woman showed signs of interest, her dark brown eyes widening.

'*Sí*. Or from the United States—I am not sure. He speaks very good Spanish,' said the nun. 'You come now to see him? He is in the courtyard. Maybe when you see him your memory will return *un poco*, hm? Dr Gonzalez says that might happen when you see someone who is familiar to you.'

The young woman rose to her feet, showing more energy than she had shown for a long time. Excitement beat along her nerves, chasing away the awful apathy. Automatically she straightened the T-shirt and skirt and patted at her hair in a pathetic attempt to improve her appearance. Had her prayers been answered at last? Was she about to find who she was and what had been her life before she had been injured in the plane crash? She knew her name was Kate Lawson and that she was a British citizen; the airline authorities had been able to supply that information. She knew also that she had been travelling with her parents who had both been killed in the crash. But beyond that she knew nothing. She remembered nothing of her life before she had regained consciousness here in the Mission hospital.

Eagerly she followed Sister Monica, the nun who had been assigned to look after her because she was the only one of the Sisters with a reasonable command of English. From the cell-like room they stepped out into the cloisters which bordered the central courtyard of the Mission building. Sunlight cast black shadows from palms and orange trees against the glowing pink stone of the building and glinted on the mosaic tiles enclosing a pool in which there stood an ornate bronze fountain. No water trickled from the fountain because since the outbreak of revolution in the small Central American State of San Marco all water had been used very sparingly in the Mission.

A man was standing beside the pool staring down into the still dark water. Of medium height, with broad shoulders, he was wearing khaki-coloured shorts, a khaki bush shirt and sandals. On his head was a shallow-crowned, wide-brimmed straw hat such as the natives of the country wore when working in the fields to protect their heads from the tropical sun.

'*Señor*, here is Señorita Lawson,' announced Sister Monica.

He turned quickly and Kate had an impression of explosive energy kept under strict control. For a moment he was perfectly still as he stared at her, his eyes gleaming brightly in the shadow of the hat brim. Then, taking off the hat, he came towards her and she had another impression of skin tanned to the colour of teak, of light grey eyes under level dark eyebrows, of shaggy dark hair slanting across a broad forehead and lapping his shirt collar before his hands reached out to her shoulders and she was drawn towards him and held closely.

'Kate, it's good to see you at last,' he said warmly, and pressed his rough, bristly cheek against hers in an affectionate caress. 'I'm Sean Kierly, your fiancé. Before you left England to come here we'd planned to get married next year,' he whispered in her ear, his breath tickling the tender skin. 'If you don't remember, pretend you do. It's the only way I'm going to get you out of this place. I promised Hugh I'd do what I could to find you and arrange somehow for your release.'

'Hugh?' she queried, tilting back her head so she could look at him properly, waiting for recognition to flood through her and with it the memory of her life before the plane crash.

'Hugh O'Connor, your mother's brother. He wanted to

come for you himself when he heard you were being kept here, but he couldn't get a visa. The chaos here has made it difficult for foreigners to enter the country.'

'Then how did you get here?' she asked.

There were tiny yellowish flecks in his eyes around the pupil and they seemed to flare like flames when his eyes widened slightly. Then he smiled at her his long upper lip curving back attractively to reveal even white teeth, thick black lashes coming together and almost concealing his eyes and her heart seemed to do a somersault. Raising a hand, he caressed her cheek with the knuckle of his forefinger.

'That knock on the head really affected your memory, didn't it, sweetheart?' he scoffed softly. 'I'm a news reporter and I was sent by the international news agency I work for to cover the rebellion here. We met at your Uncle Hugh's house in Hampstead, you and I. You're still a student at a college of music in London. You're studying piano and voice.' His smile faded and his eyes grew hard. He leaned close again, his cheek brushing hers. 'For God's sake,' he muttered in a sharp autocratic whisper, 'make some show of pretending you remember even if you don't, or they'll have me thrown out!'

'I'm so glad to see you,' she cried sincerely, and wound her arms about his neck. She planted a shy kiss upon his cheek.

'Very good. More convincing,' he murmured. 'How much English does the nun understand?'

'Enough,' she replied, giving Sister Monica a wary glance.

Releasing her he turned to Sister Monica and spoke to her in Spanish. The nun answered him in the same language, her hands moving in excited gestures. Turning to Kate, she broke into English.

'You know, *señorita*, that I can't leave you alone with him. I have orders that you are never to be left alone except when you are in your room—Señor Valdez insisted on that.'

'Valdez? You mean General Valdez, leader of the guerilla army who has just become the new President?' Sean Kierly queried sharply.

'*Si, señor*. He says it is very important that Señorita Lawson is looked after and protected for her own good.'

'I'll go and see him,' said Sean Kierly firmly. 'He'll let you leave the country when he knows our relationship, I'm pretty sure.' He stepped close to Kate again and drew her to him. 'Will you trust me and do anything that's asked of you to get out of this country?' he added very quietly, hardly moving his lips so that Sister Monica couldn't hear properly what he was saying.

Kate studied the clear cold eyes, the severe aquiline features. He was the answer to her prayers, she thought, a strong determined man, a knight errant come to her rescue.

'Yes, I'll do anything,' she replied, her hands sliding up over his shoulders, her fingers tangling again in his hair, her mouth lifting in mute invitation.

Again she saw the little flecks flare in his eyes, then his lips pressed against her mouth. Her lips trembled and parted, and he took advantage and tasted the sweet moistness of her mouth. Her senses reeled and her fingers gripped his hair. His breath mingled with hers as he muttered an oath and he lifted his head sharply. For a moment his eyes blazed down into hers before he pushed her away from him as if he daren't hold her any longer.

'Forgive us, Sister,' he said in English, smiling at the surprised and staring nun.' It's been a long time since Kate and I have been together. We are engaged to be married and recently I thought I might never see her again.' His smile widened and he made a gesture with one hand. 'You can see how it is with us. We are very much in love.'

'Is it true?' Sister Monica's eyes were round as she looked at Kate.

'Yes, it's true,' said Kate happily, and glanced shyly at Sean. 'I remember him. Oh, Sister, isn't it wonderful? I remembered him as soon as I saw him.'

'God is good in his great mercy,' said the Sister, piously crossing herself. 'Our prayers for you have been answered. Will you tell General Valdez about this when you go to see him, *señor*?'

'I will tell him and I'll be back if not today, tomorrow. Meanwhile, *hasta la vista, querida.*' Sean smiled again at Kate and her heart seemed to sing with delight as he kissed her on the cheek. 'Be prepared for anything when I come again,' he murmured.

Leaving him in the courtyard, Sister Monica escorted Kate back to her room. When the nun had left and the door was closed Kate stood by the narrow window which overlooked the dry dusty fields at the back of the Mission, her mind buzzing with excitement.

Sean. Sean Kierly. She said the name over and over to herself, hoping it would spark off her memory, but nothing happened. No images of being with the man who had just left the Mission flashed across the mirror of her memory. It remained blank.

Surely his name should mean something to her, if she was in love with him as he had claimed. Sean Kierly! it wasn't an English name. Sean was an Irish name. Kate lifted her head suddenly, gasping in surprise. How had she known that? Her shoulders slumped again and she sighed. Dr Gonzalez had said she would remember many ordinary pieces of knowledge like the names of countries, the language she spoke. It was the memory of experiences which had been wiped from her mind like a picture can be wiped from a blackboard.

She touched her lips which had been so recently kissed and her cheeks burned as she remembered how she had responded to Sean's kiss parting her lips, pressing herself against him. Perhaps her senses had recognised his touch even if her mind had not recognised his name and her eyes had not recognised his face and figure. Oh, it was all so bewildering and tormenting, it made her head ache.

Hugh O'Connor. Another Irish name? Her mother's brother, her uncle. Had her mother been Irish? She had been told that her parents had been British and had come out to San Marco a year ago when her father who had been a geologist had been sent to supervise an exploration survey for oil. She had been visiting them for a holiday and when the revolution had erupted they had been ordered to leave the country by the oil company. The plane taking them to the United States had crashed soon after take-off and had burst into flames. Thrown clear, by some chance, Kate had been the only survivor.

Springing to her feet, she paced up and down the room. The coming of Sean, while not triggering off her memory, had at least roused her out of the depression into which she had sunk. And she knew new facts about herself. She knew now she was a musician. Holding up her hands, she flexed her fingers. She played the piano. No wonder her hands were so muscular! And she sang. Opening her mouth, she sang a few notes of the hymn she had heard the nuns singing that morning. Her voice was strong and true, quite deep.

She played the piano, she sang, she was a student at a college in London and when she had graduated she was going to marry Sean Kierly. Again her cheeks burned with excitement as she thought of all that marriage meant, of courtship and the culmination of lovemaking, of learning to live with another person. She was going to do that with the forceful, dynamic man who had come to her that morning. She could see why he would be attractive to her. But what was there in her to attract him?

She wished he could have stayed longer and told her more about himself and of course about herself. But he would be back, if not today, then tomorrow, and when he came back he would take her away with him, back to Britain, to her old way of life, and maybe on the way there she would remember everything.

Sean didn't return that day but, comforted by the knowledge that someone who knew her and loved her was in San Marco, Kate slept better that night than she had done for a long while. Breakfast was over the next morning and she had just returned to her room when Sister Monica came bustling in to tell her that she was to go with her immediately to the Mother Superior's office where General Valdez, Dr Gonzalez and Señor Kierly were waiting to talk with her.

When she entered the pleasant yet severely simple room where Sister Teresa, the tall ascetic-looking nun who was in charge of the other nuns, was sitting behind her desk, Kate went straight up to Sean, smiling in greeting and lifting her face to be kissed.

'So, Señorita Lawson. We are told that your memory has come back,' said Dr Gonzalez. Grey-haired and a little stooped, he stared at her curiously. 'Sister Monica says that you recognised Señor Kierly almost as soon as you saw him. Is that right?'

'Yes.' Kate slipped her hand into Sean's. 'But I can't remember everything yet.'

The doctor turned to the man at his side and spoke to him in Spanish. General Valdez was a short broad-shouldered man of about thirty-five. He had greasy black curls and a thick black beard. He nodded his head while the doctor spoke, but all the time he watched Kate with small black eyes set close together on either side of his high-bridged nose. When the doctor had finished speaking General Valdez came forward and bowed slightly from the hips to Kate.

'I am Diego Valdez, *señorita*, and I regret I haven't had time to meet you before this,' he said in heavily-accented English which Kate found hard to understand. His beady eyes shifted from her to Sean and back to her again. 'Señor Kierly says he is your fiancé and that he has come to take you back to England. Naturally I have to be careful in this matter. I have to be quite sure he is what he says he is. What do you know about him?'

Kate took a quick sharp breath, wondering how to answer him. She glanced up at Sean. His eyes held hers and he squeezed her hand encouragingly.

'Tell him, Kate. Tell him what you've remembered,' he urged.

'Sean is a news reporter and he works for an international news agency,' she said, looking directly at the General. 'I met him in London, at the house of my uncle, Hugh O'Connor. I . . . we . . . plan to be married next year when I've graduated from college.'

'What do you study at college? Can you remember that?' asked General Valdez, his dark eyes still cold with suspicion.

'Music. I play the piano and I sing.'

'How do you sing?' demanded Valdez.

'How? I don't understand,' muttered Kate in bewilderment.

The General turned to the doctor and spoke to him in Spanish.

'The General wishes to know if you sing soprano or contralto,' explained the doctor in his slow careful English.

'Contralto,' replied Kate immediately, surprising herself because she hadn't remembered that consciously. 'Listen.' She sang a few notes of a scale.

'Very nice. Very good,' remarked General Valdez with a sneer.' But not enough. Sing a song, one you learned in England.'

She tried hard to remember a song, but her mind remained blank and the ache at the back of her head began. Her temples throbbed and she raised her hands to rub at them with her fingers.

'I can't,' she whispered. 'I can't remember.'

Upset by her inability to remember, she turned instinctively to Sean. He put his arm round her shoulders and drew her against him comfortingly.

'Take it easy, darling. Don't let him pressure you,' he told her gently.

'You are right, Señor Kierly,' said the kindly doctor.' It won't do any good to try and make her remember too much at once. It is best for her memory to return slowly and naturally.' Once again he spoke to the General in Spanish, obviously cautioning him too.

While he listened General Valdez stared at Kate again. Then his glance swept to Sister Monica who was standing with her hands folded demurely before her. Her head was bent and close beside her was the Mother Superior, who also had her hands clasped as if at prayer. Both nuns raised their heads sharply when General Valdez barked at them. Sister Monica blushed and glanced appealing at the Mother Superior, who gave the General a cold glare and went off into a scathing tirade in Spanish. Without waiting for her to finish the General began to shout at her and soon the doctor and Sister Monica were adding their voices to the argument. All four seemed to have forgotten about Kate and Sean.

'What's the matter with them? What are they arguing about?' Kate asked.

'The Mother Superior has taken exception to the way Valdez is questioning Sister Monica. She doesn't think he's showing enough respect. And he wants to know what she heard us say to each other when we met yesterday, and she won't tell him.' Sean hugged her shoulder lightly. 'You did well just now. You've convinced the doctor. But Valdez still has to be convinced. He's very reluctant to let you leave the country.'

'I wonder why?'

'Something to do with his image as the newly declared President of San Marco.' He gave her a searching glance. 'Have you remembered anything since yesterday?'

'Not really. I recognised your name as being Irish, that's all. Are you from Ireland?'

'No, not originally, but I can claim Irish blood. I was born in the States. My father, who was also a news reporter, was killed on an assignment in Korea and when my mother married again she left me with my paternal grandfather. He was a journalist too and when he retired he went to live in Ireland. I went to school there for a while.'

'You've probably told me all this before,' she whispered. 'I'm sorry I can't remember anything about you.'

'Don't worry about it,' he replied comfortingly. 'Right now all that matters is persuading this devious devil Valdez to let you leave the country with me.'

'Señorita Lawson.' General Valdez was back in front of her, his dark face set in a vicious expression, his black eyes blazing with anger. Over at the desk the two nuns were both breathing heavily and glaring angrily at him. Dr Gonzalez seemed to have given up and had retreated to a window.' You know why you have been kept in this Mission?' barked Valdez.

'Because I've been ill?' suggested Kate nervously.

'*Si*, that is true, but also for your own protection. I could not let anyone in your state of mind leave and travel to another country alone,' stated the General. Thrusting his thumbs into the wide leather belt at his waist, he rocked back and forth on his heels. 'If I had you would have got lost and then I would have been most unpopular with your government and the British people. You understand?'

'I . . . er . . . yes, I think so. But you can let me go now, with Sean. I'll be quite safe with him,' said Kate. 'Please let me go with him, *señor*,' she added pleadingly.

'On one condition,' he said melodramatically.

'And that is?' said Sean sharply.

The General looked at him, his eyes narrowed so much that they seemed almost closed.

'That you agree to be married first,' he drawled the words out.

The room was suddenly very quiet as if everyone but herself was holding their breath, thought Kate. Sean was gripping her hand so tightly that the circulation was stopping in it.

'So? Do you agree?' taunted General Valdez.

'Yes, I agree,' said Sean smoothly. 'But it depends on Kate. Would you like to be married here in San Marco before we leave?'

Kate didn't hesitate, knowing that if she didn't agree General Valdez had the power to keep her in San Marco against her will, holding her as a sort of hostage.

'Yes, of course I would like to be married to you here.' She looked up at Sean and smiled. 'We'll only be anticipating what we were going to do next year, won't we?'

The grey eyes narrowed and hardened as the dark eye-brows slanted in a frown.

'Yes, I guess so,' he drawled, and she experienced a strange flicker at the back of her mind as if a door were trying to open to show her the truth about herself and about him. He turned to General Valdez. 'Okay, we'll be married first. But how soon can it be done? I'd like to leave for Mexico today.'

'As soon as we can get a priest,' replied Valdez, and showed his teeth in a sort of snarling smile. 'It will make a good news item, hm? The world will know how well Diego Valdez treated your fiancée and then arranged your marriage. It will make me seem like a great humanitarian, helping lovers in this way, eh?' He laughed throatily.

'You'll provide a legal marriage certificate, of course,' Sean said coolly. 'It isn't possible for Kate to obtain another British passport until we reach Mexico City, and I'll have to have some sort of document to prove she is my wife when we reach the border.'

'You'll have a certificate, with my signature on it as witness. And I promise you there will be no problems at the border if you cross it in the mountains after dark!' Valdez rubbed a thumb against a finger. 'A few dollars, that is all you will need at that time of day to get into Mexico.'

After that everything happened so quickly that later when she looked back to that day Kate could never remember how she got from the Mother Superior's office to the sunlit Mission chapel. But she did remember vividly standing before the tonsured priest who made a great effort to go through the ceremony in English for her benefit, stumbling over the pronunciation of some of the words. She remembered also the confusion when Sean was asked to produce a ring to put on her finger and had none to give her. At once General Valdez stepped forward and pulling off the ostentatious gold and emerald ring he wore on his little finger handed it to Sean. Afterwards Kate had great difficulty in persuading the General to take his ring back.

Leaving the chapel, they went straight to the dusty Ford station wagon in which Sean had driven to San Marco from Mexico, and after saying goodbye to Sister Monica and the Mother Superior Kate climbed into the front seat beside Sean. As the vehicle trundled down the narrow road to San Marco city the last glimpse she had of the Mission was the rounded bell tower glowing rose-red in the sunlight, soaring up against the brilliantly blue tropical sky.

Sean drove through the shambles of the city without stopping. Among the debris of buildings destroyed in the recent rebellion men and women were working side by side to restore some sort of order. At the doors of shack-like houses thin children in ragged clothing sprawled about lethargically.

'How miserable they look! How underfed and unhappy,' whispered Kate. 'Do you think they're glad Valdez is now President?'

'It's hard to tell,' replied Sean. 'My guess is the whole place is going to erupt in civil war again in the next few days when some of Valdez's recent followers rebel against him. That's why I wanted to get you out of the country before another holocaust starts. Thank God you agreed to be married! You realise, I hope, that Valdez was testing us with that condition. He wasn't convinced your memory had returned or that I was your fiancé until we agreed to be married there and then.'

'How long will it take us to reach the border?' she asked. She was hoping that the sight of the scenery might trigger off some memory of the time she had spent in the country with her parents, but there was nothing familiar about the broad dusty highway which arrowed in front of them across a flat plateau of parched-looking land where groups of emaciated cattle grazed amongst cacti. On the horizon the shapes of mountains showed, purple where they were shadowed, glittering like gold in the sunlight.

'About three hours. We'll go on from the border to San Cristobal. It's pretty high up in the mountains, but it's fairly civilised because it's one of the oldest cities in Mexico and popular with tourists. We'll stay the night in one of the hotels and tomorrow we'll drive on to Tuxtla Gutierrez. From there we can fly to Mexico City. I'll try and get in touch with the British Embassy there tonight so they can arrange for Hugh to meet us at the airport.'

Sean spoke with cool authority. Kate glanced at him, admiring the clear-cut lines of his profile against the window beyond, and felt her pulses leap suddenly with excitement. He was a strong, dynamic person and he was her husband.

'How old are you?' she asked, and he gave her a surprised sidelong glance.

'Thirty-one.'

'I have to ask you because I can't remember,' she said apologetically.' Do you know how old I am? Dr Gonzalez said he guessed I'm about twenty.'

'You were twenty-two last birthday.'

'When was my birthday?' She was delighted because at last she was with someone who could give her information about herself. 'Did you give me a present? Did we do anything special to celebrate?'

'I didn't give you a present,' he replied, keeping his glance on the road.

'Oh. Why not?'

'Because I didn't meet you until after your birthday,' he replied easily.

'Then we haven't known each other very long.'

'We haven't known each other very long,' he agreed smoothly.

'Had you met my parents?'

'No. They were already living in San Marco when you and I met.'

'I wish I could remember what they were like,' she muttered, disappointed because he hadn't known them and so couldn't describe them to her. 'You said my mother's brother is called Hugh O'Connor. That's an Irish name too. Was my mother from Ireland?'

'Hugh is, so I presume she was too,' he said dryly. 'He'll be able to answer all your questions.' He slanted her a glance. 'Could be that when you see him you'll remember everything.'

'I hope so,' she said fervently. 'I'm so excited because I'm free again and out of the Mission. The nuns were very kind and so was Dr Gonzalez, but I felt like a prisoner there.' She leaned across and touched his thigh. 'I'm so glad you came, Sean, to rescue me.'

He took a hand off the steering wheel, covered hers with it and pressed gently. Then he lifted her hand off his thigh and placed it on the seat between them.

'We'll talk about it later, when we get to San Cristobal,' he said quietly. 'Right now I'd like to concentrate on driving.'

Kate couldn't help feeling repulsed. Leaning back, she studied his profile again. There was a ruthlessness about the set of his mouth she hadn't noticed before and she felt a strange shiver of uneasiness. She had married him, and yet she knew nothing about him beyond what he had told her.

'Have you been married before?' she asked.

'No.'

'But you've had girl-friends ... before you met me, I mean,' she persisted.

'A few.' His cheek creased attractively as he grinned.

'I wish I knew why you chose me to be the one you would marry,' she said with a sigh, and watched closely for his reaction. The crease appeared in his cheek again, not because he had smiled but because the corner of his mouth had twisted with exasperation. Against the tan of his face his light eyes glinted coldly as he glanced sideways at her again.

'Look, why don't you relax and try to sleep? This journey is pretty tedious, nothing much to see until we get to the mountains, and by then it will be dark.'

'You're annoyed with me, aren't you, for asking questions?' she accused. 'But I can't help it. I can't remember anything about you, and it worries me. It's like being married to a stranger.'

He gave her another narrowed, glinting glance, then looked ahead.

'No point in worrying,' he said tersely. 'It's done now and if we hadn't done it Valdez would have kept you prisoner in that Mission and perhaps you might never have got out of San Marco. Keep that in mind always.'

'I'll try.'

Somewhat comforted by his remarks, Kate shifted round in her seat and leaned her head against the pillar of the door. The landscape was changing now as the road swept higher through rolling foothills made up of blocks of wind-eroded rocks which were piled upon each other like giant steps, glowing rose and ochre in the brilliant sunshine. There were very few trees and not much habitation, although ahead of them, gleaming against the massive shoulder of a barren mountain, Kate saw the white walls of the houses of a small town.

The highway bypassed the town and curved deeper into the mountains. Above level ridges of rock a storm was brewing, charcoal and sulphur-yellow clouds coiling together. The atmosphere in the station wagon was heavy and soporific in spite of the air-conditioning vents being open, and Kate felt her head drop several times. Giving in at last, she turned in her seat once more and leaning her head against the upper part of Sean's arm, she went to sleep.

It was silence and the lack of movement which woke her, and for a few moments of sheer panic she wondered where she was. It was dark and she felt cold. After a while she realised she was lying down with her head on the seat behind the steering wheel.

Slowly she sat up. Through the windscreen she could see the dark shapes of mountains hunched against a moonlit sky. From the back of the station wagon came the sound of metal clinking against metal. It stopped. Footsteps crunched on stones. The door opened and Sean heaved himself into the seat behind her.

'What were you doing?' she asked.

'Filling up the tank with gasoline. There are no petrol stations on this road until we get to San Cristobal, so I had to bring a supply with me.'

She shivered suddenly and rubbed her cold arms with her hands. Sean reached over the back of his seat and rummaged around in his valise.

'Here, put this on,' he ordered, and tossed her a sweater. She noticed he was wearing a zipped jacket of thick wool over his shirt. 'Are those the only clothes you've got?' he asked brusquely.

'Yes, except for the nightgown the nuns gave me, which is in that bag Sister Monica gave me.'

'Hmm, not much of a trousseau,' he mocked lightly.

'You'll have to buy some clothes when you get to Mexico City. You can hardly travel back to England in those rags.' He put the back of his hand against her cheek suddenly. As if to check on how cold she was. 'Feeling better for your sleep?' he asked, speaking more gently.

'Yes, thank you.' In the darkness she felt more at ease with him because she wasn't able to see the hard severity of his aquiline features or the cold glint of his eyes. On sudden impulse she caught his hand and drew it across her lips, kissing it as if in homage. 'I'm so glad to be with you,' she whispered. 'You've no idea how wonderful it is to feel I belong to somebody again. Are you . . . are you glad you're with me again? Are you glad to have me back?'

His hand still against her mouth, he didn't move for a few moments, but she heard his quick intake of breath. Then his hand slid away, his fingers curving under her chin, tilting her face to his. His kiss was warm and sweet and drew from her an immediate yet shy response.

'I'm glad you're with me,' he whispered when it was over, and sliding behind the steering wheel he started the engine.

'Is it far now to the border?' she asked.

'A few more kilometres.' He swung the vehicle out on to the road. 'When we get there you don't have to do or say anything,' he added confidently. 'I'll handle it.'

Warmed by his sweater, comforted by his kiss, Kate stared ahead at the surface of the road lit up by the head-lamps. All feelings of fear and anxiety had gone and she felt calm and rested, wholly contented to be where she was, with Sean. She must love him very much, she thought dreamily, to be so happy in his company.

The Immigration and Customs post was a hut by a barbed wire fence and although lights twinkled through the windows of the hut no one came out of it even though

Sean sounded the station wagon's horn several times. After
a while he started the engine again and drove straight
through the opening in the fence and across the barren
piece of land which separated San Marco from Mexico.

The Mexican post was also an adobe hut, made to seem
a little superior to the San Marco post because there was a
flagpole in front of it. But even there the Customs officer on
duty was reluctant to leave the warmth of his hut and when
he did come he had little to say; he didn't even ask to see
Sean's passport and ignored Kate completely. He waved
them on and with a screech of tires on the stony surface of
the road the station wagon surged forward triumphantly.

CHAPTER TWO

ALMOST two hours later they entered the city of San Cristobal, the oldest settlement in the state of Chiapas, founded
by the conquistadors who had followed Cortez, and once
known as the Royal City. As far as Kate could see in the
brilliant moonlight which shone down out of a clear cold
sky, its appearance was wholly Spanish. Streets of one-
storeyed houses roofed with corrugated tiles clustered
about a central plaza.

The hotel which Sean had chosen was down one of the
streets leading off the plaza. They entered it through a
doorway set under a wide archway. Inside more stone
arches glowed in soft indirect lighting. At one end of the
foyer a fire burned in a stone fireplace. The floor was
covered with a crimson carpet. Flowering vines cascaded
down from the upstairs gallery and rubber plants and other
plants flourished in large terracotta jars set about the floor.

The smiling Mexican woman at the reception desk remembered Sean from the time he had stayed on his way to San Marco, but her smile faded when she looked at the registration card he had filled out. She glanced at Kate in surprise and said something to Sean in Spanish. He nodded and answered in the same language.

'What did she say to you?' Kate asked as they went upstairs to the gallery.

'Does it matter?' he replied casually.

'It was about me, wasn't it?' she persisted as he paused outside one of the doors opening on to the gallery. 'She didn't believe we're married, did she?'

He unlocked the door, pushed it open and went into the room, switching on the light as he did. She followed him and he closed the door.

'Does it worry you?' he queried, going across the room and putting his zipped leather valise down on the bench provided for luggage. 'That she doesn't believe you're my wife?' he added, unzipping his jacket and tossing it down.

'Well, I don't want her to think I'm just someone you picked up,' she retorted, then sighed. 'I wish I had something different to wear. Could we ... do you think we could have our meal served in here?'

'No. They don't provide room service.' He turned to her and grinned. 'You'll have to brave the stares of the curious and eat with me in the restaurant ... or go hungry. Unless you'd like me to bring you a doggy bag?'

'No, I'll brave the stares,' she said quickly. 'I'm starving. Can we go and eat now?'

'After you've washed your hands, young woman,' he mocked. 'Didn't those nuns teach you anything?'

The warmth and comfort of the hotel bedroom and adjoining bathroom, especially designed with American tourists in mind, were like heaven to Kate after the austerity of the Mission, and the meal which Sean ordered for her, beefsteak, sweet potatoes, and tiny fresh peas, was food for the gods, after a diet of rice and black beans with the occasional *taco* on which she had existed for the past few weeks.

'Mmm, that was good,' she said, when she had eaten everything that had been put before her and was sipping sweet milky coffee.

'You're too thin,' said Sean abruptly, his glance roving over her critically. 'And from now on you're going to eat as much as possible until you're back to normal weight.'

Suddenly selfconscious about her appearance again, Kate looked down at her arms. They looked like white matchsticks emerging from the wide short sleeves of the cotton T-shirt. She glanced at the next table. Some Americans were sitting there. One of them was a young woman with silky blonde hair and a smooth golden skin set off attractively by the black dress she was wearing. It had a low bodice held up by spaghetti-thin straps curving over the shoulders. Several times during the meal she had noticed Sean look at the woman and then look back at her, and now she wondered if he was ashamed of her appearance.

'What would you like to do now?' he asked.

'What would you like to do?' she replied diffidently. Compared to the two men with the American woman he was extremely handsome, young and dynamic. She looked at the other table. Yes, the young woman was looking at Sean, eyeing him up and down covetously.

'I have work to do,' Sean said sharply, as if her lethargic answer had irritated him. He tossed down his table napkin and rose to his feet. 'I have to phone through a report on the situation in San Marco to the agency's Mexican office.' With a hand under her elbow he urged her towards the foyer. Out there he put a hand in his pocket and pulled out the key to their room. He was going to give it to her when the outside door of the hotel was pushed open and two men talking noisily in American-accented English came in. At once Sean took Kate's arm again and hurried her towards the stairs, almost dragging her up them. He unlocked the door to the bedroom and she had the impression that he pushed her into it. He followed her inside and closed the door.

'I suggest you stay in here while I find a phone and make my report,' he said brusquely. 'I see the fire has been lit so you should be warm enough.'

'But how long will you be?'

'God knows. As long as it takes to get through. Maybe an hour, maybe longer.'

'What shall I do?' she whispered plaintively.

'Have a bath, wash your hair.' His glance was very critical again. 'It looks as if it needs it,' he added, and she flinched.

'We couldn't wash much at the Mission,' she said defensively. 'There was a shortage of water.'

'Well, there isn't a shortage here, so I suggest you make the most of it,' he said, and swung open the door. 'But whatever you do stay in here. I don't want . . .' He broke off and looked back at her, frowning. 'Now what's the matter?'

'You don't like being seen with me, do you?' she accused shakily. 'You're ashamed of how I look. I noticed how you kept comparing me with that woman at the next table, and just now how you hurried me out of the entrance hall when those two men came in.'

Sean let go of the doorknob and the door swung slowly shut. In two strides he was close to her. His eyes had softened and darkened with some emotion.

'That isn't the reason why I want you to stay out of sight,' he said quietly. 'Like Valdez I'm afraid you might get lost if you're allowed to be on your own. I'll try to be quick, but don't worry if I'm not back within the hour. There are a couple of paperbacks in my valise. You might find them entertaining.' He paused and his glance drifted to her mouth. 'I'm not ashamed of you, Kate,' he added in a whisper, and bending kissed her gently on the mouth. 'I have no right to be.'

Turning away, he left the room swiftly. For a while after he had gone Kate did nothing, just sat in a chair trying to remember until her head began to ache and depression swept over her. Being shut in this room was hardly different from being shut in the room at the Mission. She was still a prisoner, the prisoner of a man she didn't know. A shudder went through her and she clutched her head in her hands. More and more she was becoming sure she hadn't known Sean in England, had never met him anywhere before yesterday.

Her fingers groped in her hair. It felt sticky and thin. Sean was right, it did need washing. Slowly she stood up and went into the bathroom. She switched on the light and saw her reflection in the mirror. Her thinness was shocking, she realised that now she had seen the elegant smooth curves of the woman in the restaurant, her bones gleamed white through her skin, which was pale and patchy. There were dark hollows in her cheeks so that her cheekbones seemed to stick out below her eyes. She leaned closer. Her dark brown eyes were dull. Her hair was dull too, like reddish-brown string.

With a little moan of distress she turned away to the bath and twisted the taps on. Hurrying back into the bedroom, she took the white shift-like cotton nightgown from the small leather satchel Sister Monica had given her and went back to the bathroom which was already filling with steam. In a few minutes she was wallowing luxuriously in deep hot water, covering herself with sweet-smelling soapy lather.

She stayed a long time in the bath and had to wash her hair several times before it felt clean and silky. In front of the long mirror she dried herself, turning this way and that to look at her body critically, still disturbed because she didn't look like a bride; because her skin lacked the sheen of good health and she didn't have any curves. When she was dressed in the nightgown she didn't feel any better because it hung on her more like a shroud than a nightdress.

Having no comb or brush she searched Sean's valise and found both. Soon her hair was untangled and hanging straight down her back almost to her waist. Washing it had certainly helped it. As it dried it was beginning to glow with reddish lights.

Going back to the valise, she searched for and found the two paperbacks Sean had mentioned. She also found another book, bound in dark blue leather. As she picked it up something fell from between the pages and fluttered to the floor. She bent to pick it up and turn it over. It was a photograph showing a young woman with dark red hair held back from her face by a bandeau of black velvet. It was a picture of herself as she had been, she assumed, perhaps a few months ago, when her face had been softly rounded and her skin had possessed the bloom of a peach.

Feeling her legs shake, Kate sat down quickly on the edge of the bed and stared at the picture. She had been pretty once and her hair hadn't been straight as it was now but had waved thickly about her head and shoulders. When the photograph had been taken she had been happy, because she was laughing, her teeth glinting between generously curved parted lips, her eyes sparkling with light.

She turned the photograph over, thinking she might

have written something on the other side when she had given it to Sean, but there was no writing. She was glad he carried her picture with him, though, she decided, as she picked up the blue book again. It made her feel more sure of him.

She flicked open the book to find a place for the photograph. Every page was headed by the name of a day and its date and all the pages were written on until the middle of the book. The handwriting was bold and sloping, and she realised with a little prick of conscience that she was looking at Sean's diary.

About to close the book and put it back in the valise, she hesitated. Wasn't it possible she would find out more about herself and him if she read some of the pages? But to do that would be to pry into his secret thoughts and somehow she was reluctant to do that. She would just find a place for the photograph.

She chose the page on which he had made his last entry, July the fifteenth, almost a week ago, and despite her resolve not to read she could not help letting her glance stray over the words written there, her attention caught by the name Hugh.

'Hugh is here in Mexico City. He's been trying to get into San Marco. His niece Kate Lawson, daughter of a geologist who worked for Global Petroleum, is reported to have survived a plane crash and is being held in the Santa Rosa Mission hospital. Hugh asked me to check on whether the girl at the Mission is really Kate. He says she's five feet five inches in height, has red hair, and dark brown eyes. He has supplied photograph. If I find her I've got to get her out of San Marco and back to Mexico City by hook or by crook.'

There were a couple of empty lines and then scrawled on the next line were the words,

'I've heard of love at first sight, but is it really possible to fall in love with a photograph? It'll be interesting to find out if Kate lives up to this guy's expectations.'

Kate read what had been written several times because she was having difficulty in absorbing the meaning. At last the words made sense to her and with a little shuddering sigh she placed the photograph back in the book, closed it and returned it to the valise. Then picking up the paperbacks she got into bed.

She was lying in the dark, watching the glow of the fire fade and listening to the far-off sounds of music and laughter coming from somewhere in the hotel, wondering why Sean was taking so long, picturing him with the American woman, when the key turned in the lock of the door, and someone stepped into the room and the door closed.

'Sean?' she whispered.

'I thought you'd be asleep,' he replied. A light switch clicked and she saw his dim figure beyond the light shafting out from the bedside lamp.

'I couldn't sleep until you came. What have you been doing? You've been a long time.'

'I know. I've been talking to Bill Jains and Ted Camden, the two men you saw come into the hotel. They left San Marco soon after we did. They're correspondents with American newspapers.' He moved away into the shadows and she heard him unzip the valise. 'I think I'll take a bath,' he murmured.

The light went on in the bathroom, she saw him silhouetted briefly against it and then the bathroom door closed. She let out her breath, rolled on to her side and closed her eyes. She knew now why he had hurried her out of the foyer when the two men had entered the hotel. He hadn't wanted them to see her with him. He hadn't wanted to explain about her. He was ashamed of her. She hadn't come up to his expectations.

Groaning, she rolled on to her other side. Supposing it was true and he hadn't been her fiancé in England, and wasn't in love with her, what was she going to do? How she wished now that she hadn't looked at his diary and seen those impersonal words which suggested they had never met each other until yesterday, because she wanted to have met him in England; she wanted him to have fallen in love with her and have asked her to marry him.

When he came back from the bathroom she didn't speak, nor did she open her eyes. After a while she felt the other side of the bed sink down as he climbed into it. He settled the bedclothes and there was a click as he switched off the lamp.

With almost the width of the bed between them they lay in silence which was broken only by their breathing. The distant music and laughter had stopped. Everyone had gone home or to bed. The hotel was quiet, so quiet that Kate was sure Sean must be able to hear the thunderous rapid beat of her heart.

'Sean,' she whispered at last, unable to stand the tension any longer.

'Mmm?'

'Am I . . . I mean, do I look like I did when you knew me in England?'

He took so long to answer that she was beginning to think he had fallen asleep.

'Why do you ask?' he said at last.

'I thought that perhaps I'd lost my looks and that you're disappointed in me.' Her voice quavered plaintively although she tried hard to keep it cool and steady. Again he took his time in answering and she found herself clenching her hands in an effort to contain her emotions.

'You're different from what I'd expected,' he said

slowly, almost warily. 'But I'm not disappointed,' he added quickly.

There was another long silence. Her eyes wide open now, Kate watched moonbeams dancing on the ceiling. Turning her head, she found she could see Sean. He was also lying on his back, his profile dark against the moonlight slanting through the window. A great urge to lie closer to him swept through her and before she could stop herself she shifted nearer and nearer to him until she could feel heat emanating from his body and could smell the fragrance of soap on his skin. The silence went on, save for the pounding beat of her heart. He didn't move, yet he must have known she was closer.

Her eyes aching with the strain of trying to see in the moonlit darkness, she reached out a hand and touched his arm. It was bare, silky with hairs, the muscle tensing suddenly under her fingertips.

'Did we ever make love when we knew each other before?' she whispered daringly.

'What do you think?' he parried, and moved his arm so that her hand slid off it.

'I . . . I'd like to think that we did,' she confessed. 'And I'd like us to make love now.' She rested her cheek against the taut smoothness of his shoulder and felt him shudder as he drew in a short sharp breath.

'You've been ill and are still far from well,' he said quietly, and though he lay very still she heard his heart change gear to beat more rapidly. 'I thought we should wait until your memory comes back.'

'But it might never come back,' she sighed. 'And tonight is our wedding night.' Still he didn't move and something in her seemed to burst. Turning her face against his shoulder, she cried, 'Oh, I don't believe you like me any more and you're wishing you hadn't been forced to marry me.

Yesterday at the Mission you kissed me as if you loved me, but you haven't kissed me like that today, not once, not even after we were married.'

He moved at last, and turned towards her, cupping a hand under her chin to push it up, one bare leg thrusting between hers.

'All right,' he said tautly, 'I'll kiss you as if I love you.'

With both hands she groped for and found his head, lifting her fingers through the thick springy hair.

'Kiss me hard,' she whispered. 'Oh, wake me up and make me feel again!'

Sean muttered something unintelligible below his breath and then his lips took hers, pressing against them until the tender skin inside her mouth was torn by the sharpness of her own teeth and her breath was completely cut off.

His withdrawal was as sudden as his attack had been. Both breathless, they strained to see each other. The moonlight struck pale fire from under Sean's lashes as his glance drifted down to the simple shift which covered her.

'Kate, are you sure?' he asked, his voice husky.

'Yes, I'm sure, I'm sure!' She lifted her arms about his neck and pulled him down again. 'But I don't know how, please show me how. Show me how to love you. Show me what to do.'

His breath was sweet. His lips smiled against her brow and in her hair. Gently he took her hands, encouraging them to explore the muscle-padded curves of his body. The feel of his skin under her fingertips sent tingling suggestions chasing along her nerves to gather in a tight knot in the pit of her stomach.

Speaking softly, drugging her mind with words, he graced her glimmering face, her too slender limbs, her small breasts with his touch, and as he roused her passion his own grew stronger and stormier, became a turbulence which surged through him to swirl out and around her, sweeping her onwards to a beautiful oblivion. And suddenly, she knew with an uncanny certainty that being in Sean's arms was where she belonged.

It was the noisy clash of brazen bells which woke her from the heavy sleep into which she had fallen. At first she thought she was back at the Mission and the bells were ringing to waken the nuns and bid them to early morning prayer, and she cried out in panic.

'No, I don't want to be in the Mission! I don't want to be there. Oh God, let me not be there!'

'Hush, Kate.' A deep voice spoke in her ear and an arm curved about her waist. She was gathered against a warm pulsing body, felt a breath feathering her neck. 'It's all right, darling, you're here in San Cristobal with me, not at the Mission.'

She lay still and considered the voice. It wasn't her father speaking. His voice was lighter and spoke with a different accent. And he wouldn't be lying in bed with her.

Her eyes flew open. Rose-coloured light filtering through a window spangled the greyness of morning. She looked round. The furniture she could see was strange to her. The room she was in was not the one she had occupied in her parents' house in San Marco.

Her memory was returning, as Dr Gonzalez had said it would. She had remembered something about her father. She became aware again of the arm about her waist and the breath on the back of her neck. Who was in bed with her?

Quickly she turned her head against a swathe of red hair. It wasn't anyone she could remember being with in her life before the crash who lay there watching her with clear grey eyes ringed round with black lashes. It was the man who had come to the mission the day before and who had claimed to be her fiancé. It was Sean Kierly. She had married him yesterday and had made love with him last night.

'Did we really do it?' she whispered, shyly burying her burning face against the taut silkiness of his bare shoulder.

'We really did it,' he replied, and laughter shook in his voice. He wound his hand in her hair and slowly pulled her head up so he could look into her eyes. The mocking glint in his faded as he stared at her and was replaced by an expression of suspicion.

'What's the matter?' he asked sharply.

'Nothing, nothing,' she lied.

'Did I hurt you?'

'No, no.' She slid her hand around his neck to stroke the back of it and touched her lips to his, closing her eyes. Once she was close to him again and being enticed by his hands and lips along the sensuous path to ecstasy she wouldn't care any more that she barely knew him and had never been engaged to him.

In response to her shy kiss his lips hardened, forcing hers apart, and suddenly they were entwining again, twisting this way and that on the bed, both of them engulfed by the hot dark tide of the passion which raged through both of them.

Three hours later they left the hotel and drove through San Cristobal. In the crystal-clear mountain air the white-washed Spanish-style buildings of the city glittered. Indians wandered through the streets, mostly men, many of them wearing calf-length trousers and flat-crowned hats decorated with ribbons.

'The ribbons are all different colours,' Kate exclaimed.

'I'm told an expert can tell what group a man belongs to by the colour of the ribbons,' Sean replied. 'And they're supposed to attract the ladies, so much so that a married Zinacanteco has to tie up his ribbons while bachelors allow theirs to flow freely in the breeze.'

Delighted by this piece of folk-lore, Kate gave him a shy sidelong glance. She was still held in thrall by his love-making of that morning, her mind still insulated against the reality of the memories which were awakening within it.

'You'll have to tie your ribbons up now that you're married,' she said softly, daring to tease him and test him.

'I guess I will,' he replied coolly, and put his foot down on the accelerator as the road swept out of the city and into the mountains.

Past pyramids of rock, sparkling against the blue sky, the road to Tuxtla led and over deep ravines gouged out by swift streams, swinging gradually lower and lower until it was among coffee and banana plantations, growing in the hot and humid foothills.

In contrast to San Cristobal Tuxtla was a thriving modern city with high-rise buildings. Fewer Indians walked its streets, a fact on which Kate commented, and was told that many of the inhabitants were descended from German coffee planters.

They didn't stop in the city but drove out to the airport, and it was when she saw the planes that Kate knew she could no longer pretend that she couldn't remember what had been her life before the plane crash. Mute and miserable, she sat waiting for Sean while he returned the station wagon to the rental agency and then made reservations for them on the next flight to Mexico City.

Memories of her parents poured into her mind, as they packed bags hurriedly, drove to the airport at San Marco, boarded the small plane which was to take them to Mexico. In her ears was the terrible thunderous cracking sound of the fuselage breaking up. She shuddered and gasped, cringing within herself, and looked around wildly for Sean.

He was coming towards her, a handsome, compact man who walked with a spring in his step and looked about him with clear observant eyes, and she knew for sure that he had not been her fiancé. He sat down beside her and she studied the lean dark-chinned face, the humorously curved long-lipped mouth, the strong column of the suntanned throat rising up out of the open collar of his shirt.

'I've remembered,' she said dully. 'I've remembered my parents, Uncle Hugh, the crash—oh, God, it was awful!' She shuddered again and covered her face with her hands. 'I remember everything,' she went on. 'But I don't remember you.'

He was very quiet and still for a few seconds, then she felt his arm go about her shoulders.

'We have half an hour before our flight is called,' he said gently. 'Let's go and get something to eat and drink.'

She went with him to the small restaurant and sat at a table while he went to the self-service counter for sandwiches and coffee. When he came back he sat beside her again and passed food and drink towards her.

'Why did you do it?' she muttered after she had drunk some coffee and had nibbled at a sandwich. 'Why did you tell me all those lies about us having met at Uncle Hugh's house and being engaged?'

'I told you when we met,' he replied. 'It was the only way I could get into the Mission to see you. They wouldn't have let me see you if I hadn't claimed some sort of relationship. And even if you had been able to remember I would have done it and asked you to go along with the deception.' He paused, then laughed a little ruefully. 'But not for one minute did I think we would have to get married there and then before you'd be

crossed the border, the least you can do is be honest with me.'

'I . . . I thought I might find out the truth if . . . if . . . I suggested you make love to me,' she muttered. 'I thought you would refuse if you . . .' Her voice trembled in spite of her. 'If you weren't in love with me,' she added.

Sean drew in a sharp breath, then let it out on a crisp one-word expletive.

'You don't seem to have had much experience of men,' he remarked. 'The situation was pretty heavily loaded from the emotional point of view anyway, and I'd hoped if I stayed away from you for a hour or so it would calm things down, and you'd fall asleep.'

'I wouldn't have done it if we hadn't been married,' she whispered. 'I didn't want to believe we hadn't been engaged. I wanted it to be true that we'd fallen in love and were going to be married.'

'And so you tried to make it come true,' he finished for her, and the bitter note in his voice stung her.

'Well, you didn't have to respond,' she retorted, turning on him.

His eyes hardened and grew narrow. His mouth took on an unpleasant twist.

'Oh, I see,' he drawled. 'So what happened was my fault and I'm a heel because I took advantage of the situation, traded on your loss of memory. Okay, I'll go along with that. It had been some time since I'd slept with an attractive woman and the situation did get beyond control. So what do you want me to do now? Apologise for giving in to my baser instincts?'

His roughness rasped Kate's already quivering nerves. Clenched hand at her temples, she tried to keep back the tears of disappointment which welled in her eyes, but they brimmed and slid silently down her cheeks. Sean noticed them at once, swore softly and putting an arm about her shoulders drew her against him comfortingly.

'Listen, Kate, what happened between us last night could have happened anyway and had nothing to do with what we'd both been pretending. It had nothing to do with our having been married yesterday morning.'

'Then it meant nothing,' she sniffed.

'That isn't so. Of course it meant something.' He stroked a strand of her hair away from her cheek and tucked it behind her ear and she felt his lips brush her brow in a gentle caress. 'It meant that we're attracted to each other. We like each other and we like being together. It meant that we were glad we were free and had got out of San Marco alive. It was a sort of celebration of our escape. We were high with happiness and couldn't help expressing our happiness. Our feelings got beyond our control. It was natural and very beautiful.'

Wiping her cheeks with the back of her hand, Kate pushed away from him. He wasn't saying what she wanted to hear. He wasn't saying he had fallen in love with her as soon as he had met her just as she had fallen in love with him. But she liked what he was saying. It soothed away the shame she had been feeling.

'But if you're regretting what happened now that your memory has returned,' he continued quietly, 'you can have the marriage dissolved as soon as you get to England. . . .'

'No!' she interrupted him fiercely. 'I don't want to do that. Yesterday I made promises and I'd like to keep them.'

'You're still in some kind of shock,' Sean argued, 'after the return of your memory. Could be you don't know what you're saying.'

'I do, I do,' she insisted vehemently.

'You only think you do,' he persisted.

'No, no!' She shook her head. 'I know, not think. I know I love you and . . .'

'You mustn't say that,' he whispered urgently.' Kate, what you're feeling now will probably pass, fade away once you get back to England.'

'It won't! I won't let it. I'm going to love you until . . . until the end of time.'

'*God!*' Sean ground the word out between his teeth and thrusting his fingers through his hair leaned his elbows on the table. His broad shoulders were heaving as he breathed fast, obviously disturbed by the argument. After a few moments he lifted his head from his hands and looked round at her. His face was taut, very serious.

'Marriage has never been very high on my list of priorities,' he said, speaking carefully, choosing his words. 'In fact I could say I've never included it on the list because of the work I like to do. I won't make a good husband, Kate, because I'll never be with you for long periods of time. I like my job and I like to go where the action is, go right into the midst of trouble and try to report the truth as I see it. You've got to understand that if you don't do something about dissolving this marriage we've gone through I'm not prepared to change my way of life to fit in with yours. I won't be able to live with you all the time.'

'I won't mind . . . as long as I see you sometimes,' she argued. 'I'll have my career too. As soon as I've graduated from college I'm going to teach, and I'll be very involved in that. You see, I'm remembering now that music means as much to me as reporting news means to you.'

He stared at her frowningly for a moment, then his mouth relaxed and his eyes softened.

'A career woman, hm?' he remarked softly. 'I'm glad about that, glad you have a life of your own to live.' A voice announced a flight number in Spanish and he pushed to his feet. 'That's our flight. Come on,' he said.

Kate was frightened suddenly about going on the plane, remembering the last time and she was glad that Sean held her hand. Even when she was in her seat and he was sitting beside her she clung to his hand until the plane reached its cruising altitude above the clouds. Then he withdrew his hand from hers, undid his seat belt, leaned back and closed his eyes. For the next hour Kate sat in lonely silence while he slept, tormented by the confusing emotions caused by the awakening of her memory, staring out at the bland blue glare of the sky above a thick white band of cloud.

She recognised her uncle as soon as he came towards her in the arrival lounge at the air terminal. Tall but a little stooped with grizzled reddish hair, he showed his relief and pleasure at seeing her by flinging his arms about her and holding her closely for a few seconds.

'I guess I've brought the right girl back with me,' Sean's voice held a hint of dry humour.

'You certainly have,' said Hugh, turning to him and shaking his hand warmly. 'How did you do it?'

'Kate will tell you all about it, once you're alone,' said Sean quickly, glancing warily at the young man and woman who were with Hugh. Taking the hint, Hugh introduced them as under-secretaries from the British Embassy. They both welcomed Kate and congratulated her on her escape from San Marco.

'We have just heard that General Valdez has been assassinated and that civil war had broken out again,' said the young man. 'We have a car outside and we'd like you to come straight to the embassy Miss Lawson, if you don't mind.'

Outside the building the sunshine was still bright and hot. A long black diplomatic limousine swept up to the curb and stopped. The young man opened the rear door and indicated that Kate should get in. At once she looked round for Sean. He was nowhere in sight.

'Isn't Sean coming with us?' she asked her uncle.

'He stopped inside to use the phone,' said Hugh.

'I'm not going without him,' she said stubbornly, and he gave her a puzzled look. At that moment the sliding exit doors opened and Sean came out. He came straight over to her.

'Well, Kate, this is where we say goodbye,' he said, holding out his hand to her, changing with that one gesture from the husband and lover of the past twenty-four hours into a polite stranger.

'Why? Where are you going?' she exclaimed.

'Back to San Marco to cover the latest outbreak of hostilities.'

'But . . . you . . . you might be killed,' she whispered, her hand clinging to his when he would have withdrawn it.

'So? That's part of the course.' He shrugged slightly.

'When will I see you again?' How she wished Hugh and the others weren't there listening and watching!

'I don't know.'

'I'll write to you. Will you write to me?'

'I'm not promising anything.' He managed to pull his hand free from hers, and stared at her, a frown darkening his eyes. 'It would be best if you do as I suggested in Tuxtla,' he added quietly. 'Take care, Kate.'

'You too,' she whispered, controlling a great urge to fling her arms about his neck and beg him not to leave her.

With a few words to Hugh Sean turned and walked away into the terminal building. Blinded suddenly by tears, Kate got quickly into the back of the limousine. Her San Marco adventure was over, was becoming a memory already and the future, vague and shadowy, was beginning to claim her.

CHAPTER THREE

IT was the last day of the summer term at Netherfield Private School for Girls and the assembly hall was packed with both pupils at the school and members of their family on the occasion of the annual prizegiving. All the prizes had been presented, all the songs rehearsed by the school choir for so long had been sung, all the speeches from various dignitaries such as the chairman of the board of directors, the headmistress, the chaplain and the head girl had been spoken, and now the headmistress, Miss Forbes, a slim figure in navy blue and white who was wearing the gown and hood which indicated she was a Doctor of Literature from a well-known university, was winding up the occasion with a few last words.

Seated at the piano, Kate gazed up at the high windows of the hall through which she could see a pale blue sky across which gauzy white clouds were trailing. The rounded tops of the windows reminded her of windows in another place. Somewhere else there had been windows shaped like that through which the sun had shone brilliantly, one day in July two years ago. She looked down at the ivory and black keys in front of her and frowned. Exactly two years ago, for today was July the twenty-second, the second anniversary of her marriage to Sean.

'And now to bring this most happy occasion to an end we'll sing the school song. Miss Lawson?'

Miss Forbes was looking at her. Kate snatched her thoughts back from the sunlit dimness of the chapel at the Santa Rosa Mission in San Marco. Her fingers found the right keys automatically and the introductory bars of the school song resounded through the hall crisply and clearly, in strict time. There was a rustling of clothing as everyone rose to their feet and out of the corner of her eye Kate saw Miss Dodds, the elderly and much-loved head of the school music department, raise her arms in order to conduct the assembly through the song.

In fifteen minutes the prizegiving and speech day was over. With the cheers of the girls still ringing in her ears Kate closed the piano, collected up her music and began to make her way through rows of chairs towards the staff room. Her progress was slow because many of the girls and their parents were lingering in the hall hoping to catch various teachers and talk with them, but at last she saw her way clear to the doorway of the staff room.

'Miss Lawson—Miss Lawson!'

She turned. Sunlight shone on the smooth blonde hair of the girl who had called her.

'Miss Lawson, my father is here,' said Carol Wyman breathlessly. 'He'd like to have a word with you.'

So Barry was here again. That meant her lunch would be taken care of today and perhaps later they might go for a sail in his new yacht. It was a good way to start the summer holidays, thought Kate with a surge of high spirits. The weather was perfect for sailing.

'I'll just put my music in the staff room,' she said to Carol. 'Where will I find your father?'

'He's in the garden talking to Felicity Paton's mother,' said Carol. 'Felicity has invited me to their place in Cornwall for the first two weeks of the hols, and they're just fixing up the arrangements.'

In the staff room Kate dropped her music books on one of the leather armchairs, paid a quick visit to the toilet, tidied her now thick and waving hair with a comb and put her black Bachelor of Music gown on its hanger in the closet. Another glance in the mirror assured her that the brown summer suit she was wearing with its pencil-slim skirt and casual blazer-style jacket had been a good buy; she straightened the collar of her silky blouse, left the staff room and made her way to the garden.

It was easy to spot Barry standing by the sundial talking to Felicity Paton's parents. Slim and slight, with well groomed wavy fair hair, he looked self-assured and elegant in a grey pinstriped business suit. As soon as he saw her approaching he made some final remarks to the Patons, shook hands with both of them, kissed Carol on the cheek and came towards Kate. But though his blue eyes expressed his pleasure at this meeting with her he was very careful not to show his feelings and greeted her with a formal handshake.

'Carol said you wanted to see me,' she said as they walked slowly back towards the main part of the school building. Built at the beginning of the century, it had all the charm of an old country house and its mellow brick glowed gold in the sunshine. On either side of it the new wings which housed the science labs and the art and music rooms were much more contemporary in design, four storeys high, commanding splendid views over the South Downs and, in the distance, the sun-hazed water of the English Channel.

'That's right,' said Barry. 'How have you been since we last met?'

'Well, considering how hectic the end of term has been,' she replied. 'Aren't you pleased with Carol for winning the medal for making the most progress this year? And also for getting a prize for piano performance?'

'I'm pleased, yes. It's the first time she's shown any sign of achievement, and for that I believe I have you to thank.

You're good for her, Kate. You supply the attention and encouragement she should be having from a mother.'

'Oh, I hope you're not thinking that she was awarded the prize on my say-so,' she said. 'Miss Dodds had the final say.'

'Maybe she did, but Carol wouldn't have practised if you hadn't encouraged her.' His smile was crooked and slightly bitter. 'Give me credit for knowing my own daughter. She's a lazy little bitch, just like her mother was.'

'That isn't a very nice thing to say about her,' Kate protested hotly.

'But it's true.'

'You have to remember she has something of you in her,' she argued.

'Sometimes I wonder.'

'Barry!' she exclaimed. 'Do you realise what you're implying?'

'Yes, I do. I often have the feeling Dilys tricked me into marrying her. She slept around before and after marriage. But I didn't come today to talk about my ex-wife or about Carol,' he added. 'I came to see you, my gorgeous redhead. How would you like to come sailing this afternoon? We could have lunch first at the Harbour Lights.'

'I'd like to go very much, but I'll have to go to the flat first to change.'

'No problem. We'll go by there on our way.'

He had driven to the school in his blue Mercedes sports and was sitting in it with the engine idling when she came out of the school. He was very wealthy and he showed it. Anything worth buying and owning he had bought and owned. He was the chairman of the board of directors of a group of pharmaceutical companies which his father had established. He owned a house in London and one in the country not far from Netherfield where he trained horses for steeplechasing, and he had just bought a new yacht.

'Isn't Carol coming with us?' Kate asked, as she joined him in the front of the Mercedes.

'No. She's gone with the Patons to Cornwall for two weeks,' said Barry as he drove down the driveway to the main road. 'Do you think two weeks will give you and me a chance to get to know one another better?' he added, slanting a glance in her direction. 'Or are you off to the Continent for your vacation?'

'I'm not going away immediately, but I have made plans to go to Ireland next month with some friends who are also interested in traditional music.'

'That sounds encouraging. Can I assume, then, you'll be interested in accepting any other invitation I might offer during the next two weeks?'

'You'll just have to wait your turn!' she replied lightly, and he gave her a sharp glance.

'Does that mean I have competition?' he demanded jealously.

'I'm not sure if you would regard an elderly grand-mother who lives in the Lake District as competition, but I've promised my father's mother I'd visit her soon.'

'No, I wasn't thinking of that sort of competition,' he said, flashing her a smile. 'When do you travel north? Perhaps I could drive you up there. I have relatives there too, near Ambleside.'

'Now you're rushing me!' she rebuked him. 'Let's take one day at a time, please, Barry.'

'All right. I suppose that's better than nothing.'

Kate's flat was in an old Edwardian house that overlooked the open parkland known as The Common which lay behind the promenade in the seaside resort of Westcourt. The house had been bought by the school authorities to rent to members of the staff who did not live on the school premises. As she ran up the stairs to the second floor Kate thought over her brief conversation with Barry. She couldn't help feeling intrigued by his obvious interest in her. They had met for the first time the previous December after a school concert at which Carol had played the piano. Since then he had made a point of seeking Kate out whenever he had come to the school either to visit Carol or for a meeting of the board of trustees of which he was a member.

And now he wanted to see more of her while Carol was away. Well, she might give it a whirl. He was attractive and knew how to please a woman, and so far the difference in their ages, about twenty years, had posed no problem.

Quickly she changed into neat navy blue slacks, a white turtlenecked sweater and a navy blue kangaroo jacket with a hood. In a canvas bag she packed a change of clothing in case she became wet while sailing, then hurried back down to the Mercedes.

Within ten minutes they were entering the comfortable bar of the Harbour Lights pub, once the haunt of smugglers, which overlooked the harbour of Westcourt. Sitting on high stools at the shining mahogany counter, they ate delicious crab sandwiches and drank the local brew of bitter beer. Some of the people, all of them yachtsmen, knew Barry and greeted him as he and Kate were about to leave. He replied affably, but introduced her only as Kate.

'I hope you don't mind,' he said as they left the pub and walked along to the marina where his yacht was berthed. 'There's no need to broadcast to everyone who you are exactly . . . yet. I'm fairly well known around here and people are bound to talk about us. I'd like to keep our friendship as quiet as possible since you teach at a school in which I have a financial interest. Do you understand?'

'Yes, I do. At least I think I do,' she replied. 'Oh, what a lovely boat!'

The new boat was of Scandinavian design and was painted blue, which seemed to be Barry's favourite colour. It had laid teak decks, and stainless steel fittings. Down below there were four sleeping berths, a well-equipped galley and a toilet closet complete with shower.

They set out under engine to beat the tide which was flooding through the narrow entrance of the little harbour, but once clear of the chalky headlands which gave the harbour shelter, Barry put up the sails and stopped the engine.

'I thought we'd try for Yarmouth, on the Island,' he said.

Kate looked away across the silvery grey water of the Solent to the Isle of Wight, a hazy line of green in the distance.

'It looks a long way for an afternoon sail,' she said cautiously.

'We could always stay the night there and sail back tomorrow,' he suggested.

She looked across at him. He was watching her with speculative blue eyes. Was he testing her? Was he trying to find out if she was free and easy enough to stay the night aboard with him and possibly sleep with him?

'No, Barry,' she said firmly. 'We'll go back to Westcourt and tonight I sleep alone in my own bed.'

She could tell by the sudden petulance of his mouth that he wasn't pleased with her answer, and yet in the next moment he was smiling at her.

'You know, I was hoping you'd say that,' he replied warmly. 'I was hoping you'd turn out to be what you seem to be, a nice girl.'

Kate looked away quickly, over the side of the boat at the light-dappled water which was slapping against the hull. Perhaps she shouldn't have agreed to come with him at all. If she were really what he had hoped she would turn out to be, a nice girl, she wouldn't have ever accepted any of his invitations. And it would have been easy for her to decline them without giving a reason, without telling him she was married.

Perhaps she should tell him now about Sean. She glanced sideways at him. With the tiller under his arm, his eyes watching the luff of the mainsail, he looked happy and relaxed. No, she couldn't tell him now, not while he was enjoying himself. Later today, when he invited her to go out with him again, she would tell him.

The breeze died away, leaving the yacht at the mercy of the strong currents which swirl about that part of the Solent. The sails slatted idly, the boom creaked and the boat rocked. They drank some beer and nibbled peanuts, talked and then whistled for wind. But none came. The tide was turning, beginning to ebb, so they started the engine so they could return to the harbour.

'You'll come again tomorrow, if the weather is good?' Barry asked after they had tied the boat up in its berth.

Now was the time to tell him, thought Kate.

'I'd like to,' she began, 'but . . .'

'Good,' he put in quickly. 'I'll pick you up early. About nine o'clock?'

'But I have lots of things to do tomorrow,' she went on determinedly. 'It's Saturday and I have shopping to do, housework and washing. I can't come tomorrow.'

'Sunday, then?' Barry urged, as he finished coiling the mainsheet and laid it neatly on the deck. 'And instead of sailing I'll drive you out to Rosedene to meet my mother and have lunch. You'll love the old house. There's a music room just made for someone like you, with a grand piano and a harp my grandmother used to play.'

'Do you think you should take me to meet your mother?' she asked cautiously.

'Of course I do. I want her to meet you because I want to marry you. I wasn't going to ask you quite so soon, but it looks as if I'll have to state that my intentions towards you are honourable before you'll take me seriously. Kate, will you marry me?'

Was the boat moving beneath her feet or was she swaying slightly with surprise? She sat down suddenly on the cockpit seat and stared up at him.

'I'm not sure that I can,' she whispered through dry lips.

'Why not?' He sat down beside her and took both her hands in his. 'Do you think I'm too old for you?' he added with a touch of bitterness.

'No, it isn't that,' she said hastily. 'I don't think you're too old at all, and anyway, difference in age isn't important when two people like each other and enjoy each other's company. It's just that I'm not sure if I can marry because . . . oh, because . . . well, the truth is, Barry, I was married to someone two years ago and . . .'

'Married? I don't believe it! I just don't believe it,' he exclaimed hoarsely, dropping her hands. 'Why haven't you said so before?'

'The subject never came up before,' she replied calmly. 'I'd no idea that you were interested in me . . . in that way.'

'Good God!' he muttered, and sprang to his feet to pace across to the other side of the cockpit. He stared for a moment out at the sandbanks, which now revealed by the outgoing tide gleamed dull gold in the sunshine of late afternoon. Then he swung round suddenly to face her.

'Where's your husband?' he demanded harshly.

'At the moment I don't know where he is,' she replied dully, looking down at her hands. 'We don't live together because he's a news reporter and works for an international news agency on foreign assignments.' She licked dry lips and added, 'I haven't seen him since we were married.'

'It's not much of a marriage, then,' said Barry, and there was a note of relief in his voice as he came back and sat down beside her.

'No, it isn't, and never has been,' she said stiffly.

There was a brief silence. Water lapped lazily against the hull of the yacht. Swallows twittered as they gathered together on telephone wires. Wire halliards slapped against the metal masts of the boats in the marina as a faint breeze ruffled the water in the channel between the sandbanks.

'Why don't you end it?' Barry asked abruptly. 'It should be easy enough if you haven't lived together much.' He paused, then burst out, 'Quite frankly, Kate, I don't understand what this is all about. Why did you and he marry in the first place if you knew you were going to be separated in this way?'

'I suppose I'll have to tell you everything,' she sighed. 'It's something I've never told anyone except Uncle Hugh.'

'I don't wish to force your confidence, but I'd appreciate it if you would tell me,' said Barry, turning towards her. 'I've grown very fond of you, Kate, over the past few months, and I like to think you have a certain liking for me and can trust me.'

It wasn't easy to tell him. The story of what had happened in San Marco came out jerkily and a little incoherently, but at last it was told and again for a while they sat in silence which was broken only by the twitter of the birds and the gurgling of water still retreating from the sandbanks.

'Have you ever done what he suggested? Have you ever gone to a lawyer and asked his opinion about the legality of the marriage?' said Barry at last.

'No.'

'Why not?'

Kate didn't answer immediately but looked away across the shining wet banks to the bluish-green line of trees on the opposite side of the harbour. Sunlight glinted on spires of the old church half hidden among the summer foliage of tall elms, and across the harbour came the chimes of the church clock as it struck seven o'clock.

'I suppose I was hoping it would work out,' she said, 'and develop into a real marriage. I suppose I hoped that once we were together again . . .' She broke off.

'Only you haven't been together again,' he finished for her.

'That's right.'

'He's never come to England to see you?'

'No.'

'Surely that tells you something about how he feels.' Barry leaned towards her. 'Surely it tells you that he doesn't want to be married to you? You've been deluding yourself, hanging on to a dream of romance, hoping it would come true. I'm a little surprised that an intelligent woman like you has let fantasy take such a hold. It's time you woke up Kate, faced reality. It seems to me this marriage of yours is non-existent, possibly not legal any more. After all, it happened in a country which doesn't exist any more and whose laws are possibly not recognised in this country.'

'But it was a religious ceremony,' she said. 'We made vows before a priest.'

'And that meant something to you?'

'Yes, it did,' she whispered.

'But obviously it didn't mean anything to Kierly, or he would have been to see you by now.'

'He was going to come and see me last Christmas. He

sent me a postcard from Ireland. But he didn't come and I haven't heard from him since.'

'Have you written to him?'

'Only once, after I'd returned to England from Mexico. I sent the letter care of the news agency he works for, but I didn't get a reply, so I didn't write again.' She looked again across the sandbanks, took a deep breath and added, 'I woke up and faced reality some time ago and stopped hanging on to that particular dream. Sean means nothing to me now.'

She turned and faced him as she spoke and saw triumph leap in the depths of his eyes.

'Then may I make a suggestion?' he asked. 'May I suggest you consult a lawyer about that religious ceremony which is still making you feel bound? If you like I could take you to see Paul Holgate who handled my divorce. He's very shrewd and knowledgeable.'

'I'm not sure,' she muttered hesitantly.

'I am. I want to marry you, Kate. I want you to be free from any ties with the past so you can marry me.' Barry rose to his feet. 'But we'll talk about it on Sunday. The invitation to Rosedene still stands. Will you come?'

'Yes, I'd like to,' she said, feeling more able to commit herself now that she had confided in him.

He drove her back to the flat and dropped her off, promising to pick her up on Sunday morning at eleven o'clock no matter what the weather should be like. Kate spent a restless night. His proposal had roused memories she had believed she had smothered for ever.

Lying sleepless in bed, she relived the day Sean had come to the Santa Rosa Mission. She recalled how happy she had felt when he had told her he was her fiancé, how she had accepted him without question. She went through the marriage ceremony again and drove through the mountains into Mexico with him. Writhing with regret, she remembered the night in the hotel at San Cristobal, the tenderness Sean had shown her, her own willing and passionate response.

Unable to stand the agony of remembering any longer, she left the bed and went into the kitchen to make some tea. Sitting at the table, she tried to read, hoping that involvement with the characters in the book would prevent her from worrying about her own problems. But it was no use. She kept thinking of Sean and all that he had said to her when they had been waiting at Tuxtla airport.

How naïve she must have seemed to him when she had confessed her love for him, blurting it out the way she had in a public place, possibly embarrassing him. And how foolishly romantic! Looking back now, she could see Sean had done his best to discourage her by suggesting that what she had been feeling had been an ephemeral emotion resulting only from the dramatic situation in which they had been thrown together.

And when that suggestion had failed to deter her he had warned her about himself, and she supposed she should have listened to him instead of trying to make her dream of romance come true in defiance of reality. She should have listened and made arrangements to dissolve the marriage as soon as she had returned to England, because he had been right. The feeling had passed, her love for him had faded when he had made no effort to come and see her and hadn't even bothered to answer the one letter she had written to him.

From Mexico she had returned with Hugh to London and had lived with him, his wife Geraldine and their lively son and daughter in an old house overlooking Hampstead Heath. Going back to college, she had soon become absorbed in her music studies and although there had been times when she had felt disconsolate over the death of her parents she had recovered slowly but surely from her bereavement and also from the illness she had suffered after the plane crash in San Marco. Time had healed all wounds.

After graduating she had gone for an extended tour of Europe, taking in as many musical festivals as possible. When she had returned she had been interviewed and offered a position at Netherfield and had moved into this flat at the beginning of the autumn term. Soon afterwards, Hugh and his wife, their two children having left home, had sold the house in Hampstead and had gone to live in Dublin.

The postcard from Sean had come when Kate had least expected it, redirected from the Hampstead address by the Post Office, showing a picture of a castle in the west of Ireland. Its message had been brief.

'Expect to be in England for Christmas. Will call on you. Sean.'

Kate groaned and closed the book she had been trying to read. How excited she had been when she had received that card! It had aroused hopes which she thought had been destroyed when Sean had not replied to the only letter she had sent him. And then she had realised that he had not put an address on the card and she did not know how to tell him she didn't live any longer in Hampstead. In a panic she had written to the new occupants of the Hampstead house and had asked them to give her new address to Sean when he called there. She had received a very pleasant letter back promising that he would be given the information when he called, and she had begun to prepare for his arrival, decorating the flat with a Christmas tree and lights, refusing all invitations to go and spend Christmas with relatives, sure that she would be spending Christmas Day with Sean. But he hadn't come, and she hadn't heard from him again.

Her pride had asserted itself, rescuing her from the abyss of desolation and disappointment. Once again she had been determined to forget him and had pretended to herself that she had never known him and had never married him. What had happened in San Marco and later in Mexico had been wiped from her mind, or so she had thought until today.

Barry's proposal had surprised her. She hadn't realised their friendship had progressed so far. There was much about him that attracted her. He was quiet and cultured; he appreciated music as much as she did and she sensed he had been hurt by the failure of his first marriage and so was cautious in his approach to women. He didn't want to be hurt again. Well, neither did she. So possibly they would make a satisfactory married couple, neither expecting too much of each other. Satisfactory! Kate made a face. Nothing romantic about that. She knew of many satisfactory marriages and had noticed that there was a limpness about them which did not appeal to her. But then romance was just a dream, wasn't it? As ephemeral as a summer flower, fading fast when love was not returned.

She went back to bed and fell asleep almost at once. Next day she spent lazily as she unwound and relaxed after her first year of teaching. She went to bed early and by the time Barry called for her at eleven o'clock on Sunday morning she was looking forward to seeing Rosedene and meeting his mother.

Both the house and Mrs Wyman lived up to her expectations. Situated on the outskirts of the small village of Winsteed behind the chalk downs, the house was of Regency design, the centrepiece of a landscaped park. Barry's mother was a small pretty woman with a pink and white complexion and greying fair hair. She welcomed Kate

pleasantly but with no special attention. There were other
guests for lunch, which was eaten in the long dining room
overlooking a stone terrace where two peacocks strutted
about showing off their magnificent iridescent tails.

It wasn't until after lunch when he was showing her
around the well-kept stables where his thoroughbred hunters stood in their stalls that Barry referred to his proposal.

'You've had time to think about it,' he said. 'What have
you decided to do?'

'I'd like to see your lawyer.'

'Tomorrow?' he asked, pushing the advantage immediately.

'So soon?' she parried.

'Meeting him won't commit you to anything,' he
argued. 'But it will clear the way for you to make a proper
sensible decision. You have to find out whether the marriage which took place between you and Kierly is still legal
or not. You can do nothing else until you do. And I think
the sooner you know the better for your peace of mind—to
say nothing of my own.'

'I suppose you're right,' she admitted with a sigh.

'Then you'll let me drive you to London to see Paul
tomorrow?'

'Yes, please.'

Paul Holgate was a tall man with a narrow pale face.
Behind his spectacles his eyes were like two polished grey
stones. Through the strands of brown hair which were
swept sideways across it his skull shone pink. He read the
marriage certificate which General Valdez and the Mother
Superior at Santa Rosa had witnessed two years previously
and then shot sharp questions at Kate. Soon he knew about
what had happened in San Marco.

'It was a legal ceremony,' he announced curtly. 'But

considering the circumstances under which it was performed you won't have too much trouble in getting a divorce.' His mouth twitched into a smile as he looked across at Barry. 'You could have both ignored it and gone ahead and married, but since there's the possibility of Kierly turning up and claiming that Miss Lawson is his wife I wouldn't advise it. You'd be accused of bigamy then.' He looked back at Kate. 'Any idea where Kierly is?'

'No.'

'Does she have to know?' asked Barry. 'Can't it be arranged without?'

'I would prefer to know where he is so that we can contact him and ask him to agree to divorce by consent,' said Paul Holgate seriously. 'The whole business will be over much quicker that way.' He gave Barry another shrewd glance. 'But you, my friend, had best lie low until it's all over. In fact I suggest that you get out of this office now, while I talk to Miss Lawson. And keep your meetings with her to the minimum until the divorce is through.'

Barry left the room reluctantly after making arrangements to meet Kate later for lunch at a well-known restaurant. As soon as the door had closed behind him Paul Holgate began to bombard Kate with more questions.

'Is there any way you can find out where Kierly is?' he asked.

'The news agency might know.'

'And the name of the agency?'

She told him, and picking up the phone he spoke to his secretary, instructing her to find the telephone number of the agency's London office. A few seconds later the phone buzzed and Paul picked it up again. It seemed that his secretary had contacted the agency and soon Paul was asking someone at the other end of the line if they knew of Sean's whereabouts. After a few more searching questions and a few noncommittal grunts he hung up.

'They don't know where he is. He hasn't worked for them for over six months,' he said curtly. 'So where do we go from here? Is there anyone . . . a relative or a friend who could tell you where he is?'

'I could ask Uncle Hugh. He used to know Sean before the business in San Marco. I could write to him and ask him.'

'Could you phone him?'

'No. He doesn't have a phone. He's a writer and he doesn't like being disturbed by it.'

'So it looks as if that's as far as we can go today,' said Paul Holgate. 'Will you write immediately and let me know as soon as you have information?'

'Yes, I will,' said Kate, rising to her feet. 'But supposing we can't find Sean? What then?'

'It depends on what you decide,' he replied. 'If you still want to go ahead and divorce him we can arrange something.'

Kate wrote to Hugh that night. She made no mention of Barry, nor did she say anything about divorce. After telling Hugh she hoped to be in Ireland during August attending a couple of folk song festivals as well as the annual festival of traditional Irish music which was being held that year at Ennis, in County Clare, she asked if she could call on him in Dublin before returning to England. In an offhand way she finished the letter by asking him if he had heard anything of Sean lately.

She posted the letter next day and the day afterwards left for the Lake District to stay with her father's mother in the cottage near Derwentwater. While she was there Barry found a reason to visit the district too and they spent some pleasant days together walking among the hills. After Barry returned south Kate stayed on for another week.

When she returned to Westcourt she fully expected to find a letter from Hugh waiting for her. But there was none. The only letter of importance was from the head-mistress of Netherfield saying that Miss Dodd, the head of the music department, had been taken ill and would not be returning to the school in September. As a result the position had been advertised and it was hoped that Kate would apply for it. Mrs Forbes intimated that there was a good possibility of Kate getting the job since the school authorities were very pleased with her work during the past year. Interviews of applicants would be held on the first day of September starting at ten o'clock in the morning.

Still hoping that she would hear from Hugh before she left for Ireland, Kate sent in her application for the position and then began to prepare for her trip. She and the friends from the music college who were going with her intended to fly to Dublin and hire two cars so that they could tour the southern part of Ireland on their way to Ennis.

To her relief Hugh's letter arrived the day before she left Westcourt. It was headed by a strange address in the west of Ireland. As usual he wasted very few words.

'Staying here for a short fishing holiday. Will be de-lighted to see you. After the festival at Ennis come here. Take the coast road to the village of Kilburke and ask for Moyvalla House. I hope to have an answer to your final question when you arrive. Hugh.'

That meant he hoped to know of Sean's whereabouts by the time she arrived, she was sure. Immediately she wrote to him at Moyvalla House telling him the day she expected to arrive there.

Later over dinner at the Harbour Lights she told Barry of Hugh's letter.

'So you make progress slowly,' he said thoughtfully. 'I can't help wishing Paul wasn't so sticky about wanting to contact Kierly before doing anything else. Supposing you do find him and ask him to consent to a divorce and he refuses? What will you do then?'

Kate studied the white wine in her glass. It had never occurred to her that Sean would refuse. After all, he had been the first to suggest that the marriage should be dissolved. Marriage was not high on his list of priorities, he had made that very clear by keeping away from her during the past two years and by not writing to her.

'I don't know Sean very well,' she said, 'but I do know he doesn't like being married to me. I'm sure he won't refuse.'

'If you find out where he is, will you go to see him?' was Barry's next question. He seemed rather disgruntled about something and spoke truculently.

'What's the matter? Surely you're not jealous of him?' Kate couldn't help teasing him and watched him flush uncomfortably.

'You're damned right, I am,' he said. 'Are you going to answer my question?'

'I won't be going to see him. Chances are he'll be abroad anyway, in a place where there's trouble of some sort. He likes to be in the thick of things,' she said dryly. 'The divorce can be arranged without us meeting.'

'Thank God for that,' said Barry tautly. 'Do you have to go to Ireland? Couldn't you spend the rest of your holidays here? I could take some time off and we could cruise over to Brittany and back.'

'That sounds delightful, but the trip to Ireland has been planned for some time and I've been looking forward to the festival,' she said. Then seeing he was frowning she leaned forward and said with a smile, 'Are you afraid the fairies will steal me while I'm over there, like they stole little Bridget in William Allingham's poem? *They stole little Brid-*

get For seven years long; When she came down again Her friends were all gone.' Kate broke off, seeing his frown deepen. 'Oh, don't worry, Barry. I'll be back. I have to be back by September the first.'

'Why? What for?' There was a note of possessive demand in his voice which she had heard before. He spoke to her as if he had a right to know, and she could feel resentment rising in her.

'The interview is on that day,' she replied coolly.

'What interview?'

'For the position of head of the music department at Netherfield. You must know that Miss Dodds has had to resign through ill health.'

His frown increased and his lips pursed together. He looked very irritated.

'Surely you're not considering applying for the job?' he rasped.

'I have applied,' she said serenely.

'But . . . but you're too young for a position like that. You haven't enough experience,' he exclaimed.

'Miss Forbes doesn't think so. In fact she has suggested that I apply. I think she would like me to be appointed. And nothing ventured, nothing gained. I'm really excited about it.'

'I can see that. You're more excited about that, apparently, than you are about the idea of being married to me,' he complained. 'I had no idea you were so ambitious.'

'I'm not really, but I do enjoy working at Netherfield and I know I'm as capable of organising the music department as anyone else. I have the right qualifications, I relate well to the girls and I fit in with the rest of the staff there.'

'But a job like that will make a lot of demands on your time,' he argued. 'You won't be as free as you are now.'

'May be it will,' she shrugged. 'I won't mind. The busier

I am the better I feel.'

'I won't see as much of you,' Barry went on.

'Aren't you worrying needlessly?' she retorted laughingly. 'I haven't got the job yet!'

'That's true,' he said slowly. 'You haven't.'

'Can we go now?' said Kate, rising to her feet. 'I'd like to go to bed early because we're off at the crack of dawn to catch a plane to Dublin.'

'Yes, of course.' He rose to his feet too.

He drove her back to the flats and as she was about to leave the car he put a hand on her arm. She turned and he leaned forward to kiss her on the lips. It was the first time he had kissed her and she let him do it to find out if he awoke any response in her. But he lit no flame, sent no tingles of delight dancing along her nerves, and as she made her way up to her room she acknowledged to herself that though she liked Barry there was no danger of her falling in love with him.

CHAPTER FOUR

RAIN, grey slanting curtains of it, blew sideways across a patchwork of greyish-green fields, hedges and broken down drystone walls. It had been raining, so it seemed to Kate, ever since she had arrived in Ennis four days ago, and now she was beginning to wonder why Hugh had come to stay in this wild land of the west coast of Ireland.

Yet in spite of the rain she had enjoyed the festival at Ennis. Performances by Gaelic choirs as well as by local folk singers had been of a high quality. And there had been plenty of 'off-the-record' performances too in the local pubs during the evenings by various groups, singing songs to the accompaniment of guitars, accordions and penny whistles and sometimes fiddles. Kate had enjoyed also the tour she and her friends had made of the southern counties. Driving down from Dublin through the green hills of Wicklow, they had visited potteries at Arklow, then had gone on to Waterford, famous for its glass. In County Cork they had, of course, visited Blarney Castle and had kissed the stone, and then had visited the dungeons and the bedroom of Lord Blarney, whose pleasant but evasive answers were believed to have led Queen Elizabeth I to add his name to the English language.

From Cork they had gone on to the town of Killarney, leaving their cars in the crowded town to ride in a two-wheeled jaunting car along the leafy twisting lanes of the famous yet little advertised Vale to see the three lakes. There had been no time to visit the Dingle Peninsula and view the Blasket Islands because they had to press on to Ennis for the festival, and now she was truly off the beaten track, Kate thought with a grin, as the car swept round another hairpin bend on a road which often seemed to hang precariously over the sea.

Kilburke had been nothing more than a few cottages and one pub, and she had been told there that the distance to Moyvalla House was between ten and twelve miles. According to the mileometer she had come more than thirteen miles and yet there was no sign of a house. Kate's grin widened. Of course, they were Irish miles and everyone knew they were longer than any other sort of mile.

The road plunged suddenly downwards and she had to change gear quickly to prevent the car from hurtling at high speed down a steep incline. Right to the edge of the shore the road dipped and then swooped up again like a roller coaster, and there at last was a sturdy stone wall to the left. Another quarter of a mile and she came to a gate in the wall. Beyond the gate a driveway wound between thick bushes of rhododendron and laurel.

She got out of the car, sloshed through puddles, opened the gate, went back to the car and drove into the driveway. She sloshed back to close the gate. With visions of a warm welcome from Hugh filling her mind's eye she drove on along the driveway. There would be tea, of course, because Hugh lived on the stuff, and maybe there would be scones or crumpets soaked in butter. There would be a peat fire glowing in a hearth and later there would be a comfortable bed in a pretty room.

The driveway curved into a cobbled yard of a house which was long and low with rough white walls beneath the thickness of a thatched roof. The front door was broad and arched at the top of three shallow steps.

Kate pulled at the old-fashioned doorbell, sheltering from the lashing rain as best she could. She could hear the bell pealing through the house and after a while, when the door didn't open, she rang again. The door didn't open and no lights went on. She turned the doorknob and to her relief the door opened.

The hallway was wide with a low beamed ceiling and walls roughly plastered and painted cream. A grandfather clock ticked away in one corner and as she stood hesitating, water dripping from her soaked raincoat on to the shining red tiles of the floor, the hour chimed. Six o'clock.

'Cooee! Anyone at home?' Her voice echoed back to her from the shadowy stair well. 'Hugh, I'm here! It's Kate, all the way from London to see you!'

Only the wind moaning eerily in a chimney and the patter of rain on windowpanes answered her.

Where on earth would Hugh go on a day like this? Fishing? Possibly. She wandered into the first room on the right. It was furnished as a study-lounge with big arm-chairs and a couch, a wide desk covered with papers, a pretty rosewood cabinet with glass-fronted doors and several bookcases jammed full of books and magazines. Through the two windows, set close under the eaves which came down over them, she could see the clouds, black and heavy with water vapour, billowing across a livid, wild sea.

'Hugh? Where are you?' she called again, and leaving the lounge went in search of a kitchen. She found it at the end of the hall. It was a long wide room with a flagged floor. Its ceiling was also heavily beamed and it was furnished with a table, old wooden settles, a black oak dresser loaded with blue and white willow pattern dishes, but although the place was clean and tidy there was no one in it.

Shivering, hoping that she wasn't developing a cold, Kate went back to the lounge. The fireplace was made of stone. It was deep and wide. Kindling and paper had been set in the cast-iron dog grate and on the hearth there were turfs of peat, neatly piled. On the stone shelf above there were matches, a small tub of paper spills and a man's tobacco pipe. The sight of the pipe comforted her. It meant that Hugh did live here and he couldn't be far away.

She went out to the car for her suitcase. When she returned to the house she took off her raincoat and hung it on the hallstand, noting as she did a wide-brimmed hat of dark brown tweed. Another indication that Hugh lived in the house?

In the kitchen she made herself some tea and helped herself to bread, butter and slices of ham from a shank which she found in the larder. All the time she was eating she hoped the back door would open and Hugh would appear carrying his fishing rod. But he didn't come, and by the time she had lit the fire in the lounge and was sitting on the couch watching the turfs smoke sulkily while she shivered she had to admit she was beginning to feel anxious.

She chose a book to read and wrapped herself in the hand-knitted brightly coloured afghan blanket which covered the back of the couch. Soon her head was nodding and her eyes were closing. Giving in, she dropped the book, curled up against the corner of the couch and cuddled in the warmth of the blanket she went to sleep.

She was wakened by something moist touching her cheek. A man's voice issued a soft order and the moist something went away. There was a snuffling sound followed by a whine. Kate opened her eyes and looked straight into the enquiring brown eyes of an Irish setter puppy which was sitting beside the couch. Behind it in the grate the turf fire was burning brightly so that the dog's hair, more red than her own, seemed to sparkle with ruby lights.

Remembering where she was, she sat up quickly, the afghan falling away from her shoulders, and caught sight of slippered feet resting on a footstool. The feet were attached to legs clothed in tweed trousers. Her glance shifted higher to an oatmeal-coloured Aran sweater and up to a lean, long-jawed face in which greyish-yellow eyes were as cool and still as mountain pools.

'Hello, Kate,' Sean drawled, and set down the tumbler of twinkling Waterford glass from which he had been drinking whisky.

Her breath came out in a long shaky sigh and her hands went up to her hair which had fallen down from the knot into which she usually tied it on top of her head and was straggling about her throat and shoulders.

'How long have you been here?' she asked, forcing her voice to coolness.

'Six weeks.'

'I mean how long now, this evening?' The room had darkened while she had slept, she noticed. Only one of the standard lamps had been switched on.

'About fifteen minutes, long enough to mend the fire and fix a drink.' He swung his feet off the stool and stood up. Picking up his empty glass, he went over to the rosewood cabinet. 'Can I get you something?' he asked politely. 'There's whiskey, sherry, brandy .'

'I'll have a brandy,' she said defiantly. She needed something strong to help her recover from the shock of seeing him so unexpectedly.

He brought her a goblet half full of golden liquor and went back to the armchair. She noticed he was limping, not much, but definitely favouring his right leg. He sat down, swung his feet on to the footstool and raised his glass.

'*Slainte*,' he said, giving her the old Gaelic toast.

'Cheers,' she answered.

She sipped her brandy and studied him through droop-ing lashes. Nine years older than herself, he would be thirty-three now. Not too tall, wide-shouldered, deep-chested and aquiline-faced, he was built for endurance and his shaggy hair was still black, shimmering here and there in the lamplight with blue glints, like the wing of a starling.

'Where's Hugh?' she asked.

'Hugh?' He stared at her blankly. 'Well, I suppose he's in Dublin.'

'Oh. Then why did he invite me to come here?' she exclaimed.

'He invited you to come here?' he repeated, obviously as puzzled as she was. 'Did he tell you I was here?'

'No. That's what's so puzzling. When I wrote to him telling him I'd be coming to the music festival at Ennis I asked him if he knew where you were. In his reply he invited me to come here. He didn't mention you at all.'

Sean stared at her from under frowning eyebrows for a moment of silence. Then he laughed shortly.

'Ha! Seems he's getting tired of manipulating imaginary characters for his novels and has gone in for manipulating real people,' he drawled dryly. 'He didn't tell me he'd invited you to come here.' He drained his glass and set it down. Then he patted the setter's head where it rested on his knee. His eyes glinted mockingly as he looked at her. 'So here we are, you, me and Padraic, all by ourselves,' he added softly. 'Are you going to tell me why you asked Hugh where I was?'

Disturbed by the knowledge that she was alone with him in the house, Kate gulped down some more brandy. It seared her throat and she almost choked.

'So I could tell . . . I mean, so I could get in touch with you. I asked the news agency where you were and was told you hadn't worked for them for over six months,' she said. 'What happened?'

'I took a leave of absence,' he replied curtly.

There was a short silence. A turf fell in the grate, sending up a flare of orange sparks. Kate glanced sideways at Sean. He was staring at the fire and his face was set in hard lines.

'Have you been in Ireland all that time?' she asked.

'Yes.' He stroked the setter's head again and gave her a wary look. 'I came over here from Bolivia last December. My grandfather had died and as his only heir I had to settle his business affairs. I sent you a card. Did you get it?'

'Yes.' She finished the brandy and set the glass down on the coffee table. 'Why didn't you come at Christmas?'

'I couldn't.'

'Then why didn't you let me know you couldn't?' she demanded hotly, the brandy fumes seeming to flare up in her head.

'It wasn't possible. I've told you I had to attend to my

grandfather's business affairs and when I was in Dublin I met an old friend of mine. She invited me to a party and afterwards . . .' He broke off, his face twisting in an expression of pain. He raised a hand to his forehead and rubbed at it with his fingers. The oath he uttered was crisp and expressive of some deeply felt irritation.

'She?' Kate queried, raising her eyebrows.

'Yes, she,' he retorted, not looking at her. 'From the party I drove her back to the place where she lived. After that things got out of hand somehow and I don't remember much. . . . What's the matter?' He looked round sharply.

Kate had sprung to her feet, her temper blazing up out of control, ignited by a spark of fierce jealousy.

'Don't bother to try and remember, I can guess what happened, she seethed, and stalked across the room to the hallway.

'Where are you going?' Sean demanded, lunging up out of the armchair, kicking aside the footstool and limping after her.

'I'm leaving!' she spat at him, turning to face him.

'Why?'

'I . . . I . . . can't stay here alone with you. I can't think why Hugh invited me to come here if he isn't here, but since he isn't here I'm not staying.'

'And I can't think why he didn't tell me he'd invited you to come,' Sean flung back at her, his own temper flaring up, the little flecks in his eyes blazing yellow. 'I might have cleared out if I'd known you were coming.'

'Oh—that does it!' Kate raged, and rushed out into the hall. She grabbed her raincoat, pulled it on and scooping up her suitcase she went out through the front door, slamming it behind her. Rain beat down on her uncovered head as she ran through puddles to the car. She threw her case into the back seat, and slid in behind the steering wheel. She turned the key in the ignition, but the engine didn't start.

It didn't even cough. Several times she turned the ignition, but nothing happened. She tried the windscreen wipers, the lights, with the same result: nothing. The battery was dead. Damn and blast!

Now what should she do? Rain and darkness were fast blotting out the scenery, but a shaft of yellow light was slanting out from the house through the front door which was now open. Sean was coming down the steps. Suddenly he slipped and fell. In a flash Kate was out of the car and running to him.

'What happened? What did you do?' she cried, bending over him.

His answer was to swear softly and succinctly as he tried to get up, but when she would have helped him he pushed her away.

'What's wrong with your car?' he growled when he was on his feet.

'The battery is dead. You wouldn't have a way of boosting it, would you?'

'No, I wouldn't. I haven't got a car.'

They stood facing each other, rain streaming down their faces. Kate looked away first, in the direction of the car.

'I don't know what to do,' she muttered.

'As I see it you have one alternative,' Sean said coldly. 'You can swallow your pride and stay the night here, or you can walk to the village and stay at one of the pubs.' Turning away, he limped slowly up the steps and disappeared into the house, leaving the door as if he expected her to follow.

Chewing her lower lip, Kate stayed where she was in the rain, shivering as water dripped from her hair to trickle down her neck inside the collar of her raincoat. She was regretting now the impulse which had sent her scurrying away from the warmth of the fire into the wet darkness. But as always she was finding it hard to go back on impulse. In running from the house she had been running away from something she didn't want to face. She had been running away from a discussion with Sean which would lead to them breaking up their fragile relationship for ever.

But she knew that discussion would have to take place. Now that she had made contact with him she would have to tell him about Barry and sound him out on the matter of divorce: After all, that was why she had asked Hugh if he knew where Sean was. But why hadn't Hugh told her Sean was here? Why had he let her find out in this way?

Another violent shiver shook her from head to foot and she sneezed twice.

'Kate!' Sean was in the doorway, the setter at his heels its plumed tail wafting back and forth. 'Don't be any more of a fool than you can help. You can't walk to the village in this downpour. Come inside. You'll catch your death if you don't.'

'As if you cared!' she shouted back at him.

'For God's sake——' he growled, and came down the steps in a limping run. Before she could move he wrapped his arms around her. She stiffened, throwing her head back to glare at him. She could feel anger throbbing through him.

'What are you going to do?' she challenged.

'This.' His mouth came down on hers and held it, though she tried to twist free. His lips were hot and ravenous, bruising the softness of hers. There was no mercy in the kiss, no affection or warmth, only demand. It assaulted and insulted her and she swayed under its savagery, her hands going out to thrust him away.

'Let me go!' she panted, pushing hard, without any

success. Without answering her, Sean picked her up easily and carried her up the steps into the house. He set her down in the hallway and she stepped away from him warily when she saw the anger leaping lividly in his eyes.

'Go upstairs and get out of those wet clothes,' he grated between his teeth.

'No! I'm not staying and I . . .'

'You'll do as you're told,' he interrupted her, advancing. 'Want me to carry you up and dump you in the bathtub myself?'

'No, I don't.' Kate wiped her hand across her mouth. 'You have no right to order me about! No right to kiss me either, as if . . . as if . . . *atishooo!*' The sneeze seemed to take the top of her head off and her eyes streamed uncontrollably.

'The bathroom is at the top of the stairs,' said Sean in a tightly controlled voice. 'Fill the tub with hot water and get in it. I'll go and fetch your case.'

'But I don't want to . . .' she began, and sneezed again. Ignoring her, he limped out of the front door.

It was still in her to defy his order, but she was beginning to shiver again and the thought of a hot bath and a warm bed afterwards was very attractive. Almost before she realised it she was climbing the stairs.

The bathroom had been made from what must have once been a bedroom, because it was very spacious. Hugh hadn't bothered to modernise it and the bathtub was made from porcelain-covered cast-iron, standing freely on four claw-shaped feet. Kate half expected the plumbing to be faulty, but shen she turned the taps water gushed out of both of them.

She was lying full length in the comforting soft water when the door was pushed open and Sean came in. He laid her nightgown and dressing gown on the chair and then glanced down at her, his narrowed gaze roving over

her white water-blurred body. Hating him for his inso-
lence, she stared back at him, willing herself to stay still and
brazen out the moment.

'When you're through hop into the bed in the next
room. I've put the electric blanket in it and it should be
warm by then,' he said coolly, swinging away to pick up
the clothing she had dropped to the floor. 'I'll hang these
wet things on the rack in the kitchen.'

'Thank you,' she muttered ungraciously, but he had
already gone.

In the bedroom, which was comfortably furnished with
a fluffy sand-coloured carpet and orange and brown chintz
at the dormer window, she climbed into the high fourposter bed, grateful for the warmth which had been spread
over the sheets by the electric blanket. Her head was heavy
and her throat was raw. Her sinuses were blocked too, and
she had to admit to herself that bed was the best place for
her to be that night.

Her eyelids were drooping when she heard the doorknob
rattle. At once she was on the alert. Turning her head, she
watched Sean enter the room slowly. He was carrying a
mug which steamed. He came across to the bed and set the
mug down on the bedside table.

'Drink that. It should help,' he said. Rain still sparkled
on his sweater, but he had brushed back his damp hair, and
seeing him now in a better light Kate noticed there were
threads of silver in its darkness, growing back from the
temples.

'What's in the drink?' she asked, eyeing him and then
the mug with suspicion.

'Whiskey, lemon, honey. Nothing that will harm you.
Drink it while it's hot.'

She didn't move, hoping he would go away, but he
continued to stand there watching her.

'You didn't have to make a drink for me,' she croaked hoarsely.

'I know I didn't have to, but I have. I'd do the same for anyone who had a cold,' he replied. 'Come on, show your gratitude by drinking it.'

She eased herself up and picked up the mug. The bitter-sweet hot liquid seeped past the rawness in her throat and trickled down inside her.

'All of it,' ordered Sean as she went to put down the half full mug.

'Sean, I don't want . . .'

'Drink it, or I'll pour it into you.'

She gave him a furious rebellious glare from under her eyebrows, but she drank every drop, knowing that he would force her to drink it if she didn't, and she was afraid of what might happen if she let him touch her again.

She put the empty mug down on the bedside table and slid under the bedclothes.

'Sean, I have to talk to you.'

'Not now.'

'Yes, now,' she argued.

'You can hardly speak, your throat is so sore. Best if you settle down and go to sleep.'

'But I don't want to go to sleep,' she insisted, even though she could feel drowsiness sweeping over her. 'What did you put in that drink?' she demanded thickly.

'I've told you,' he replied smoothly, and picked up the mug. 'Go to sleep. We'll talk tomorrow.'

'I'm leaving tomorrow,' she retorted defiantly, trying hard to keep her eyes open. 'We must talk now. I told Barry I'd try to contact you. That's why I wrote to Hugh and asked him if he knew where you were.'

'Barry? Who's he?'

'Barry Wyman. He . . . he's asked me to marry him.'

There, it was out at last, and Kate felt as if a great weight had been lifted off her. Now at last she could go to sleep.

'Has he now? Isn't that interesting?' he drawled. 'But what has it got to do with me?'

'You know very well what it has to do with you!' she spluttered. 'I'm still married to you, so I can't marry him.'

'Still married to me, eh? I'd have thought by now you'd have had the marriage dissolved. Okay, we'll talk about it tomorrow.' Sean clicked off the bedside lamp and she heard him go to the door. 'Goodnight,' he murmured.

'Goodnight,' she mumbled. Her eyes closed and she fell asleep.

It was daylight when she wakened. Through the window she could see a sky of washed-out blue. The rain had stopped and soft hazy sunshine slanted into the room. Her head felt heavy, but the soreness had gone from her throat. It was warm and cosy in the bed and she had no desire to get up. Slowly she stretched her legs apart, and her left leg came into contact with another leg, warm and hard. Pulling back her leg sharply, she turned her head. Sean was lying beside her, facing her, and he was looking at her with half-closed eyes.

'What are you doing in this bed?' Kate gasped foolishly, and his mouth twitched into a grin.

'Nothing very much.' He yawned, turned on to his back and stretching his bare arms above his head, let them flop down beside him. 'Until a few seconds ago I was sleeping. Now I'm waking up.'

'Who said you could sleep with me?'

'I seem to remember it was the priest who married us,' he drawled lazily, turning on to his side again. 'And this happens to be my bed,' he added, his glance roving over her. Picking up a coil of her hair which lay against her bare shoulder, he began to twist it round his fingers.

'You should have told me that last night,' she scolded him.

'Why?'

'I wouldn't have got into it if I'd known. I'd have slept in another room.'

'But it was much easier to let you sleep here,' he pointed out, pushing himself up on one elbow so he could lean over her. 'The other beds in the house haven't any sheets or blankets on them. How's the cold?'

'My throat doesn't hurt any more, but my nose is still stuffy,' she replied stiffly. Being close to him in the warm bed was dangerous and she didn't like the way he was looking at her, or the way he was pushing the sheet away from her breast or the way his fingers were sliding under the strap of her nightgown. 'We haven't seen each other for over two years,' she whispered, her hand on his trying to pull it away.

'I had noticed,' he murmured, pushing up on an elbow and leaning over her. 'I warned you I'd make a rotten husband, didn't I?'

'So you shouldn't have assumed that you can still sleep with me,' she argued desperately, struggling to resist the insidious magic of his fingertips as they stroked her nightgown away from her breast. 'No, Sean, please,' she groaned as his mouth hovered close to hers. 'I don't want to.'

'I do,' he whispered. 'I want to very much.'

'But it's not right,' she protested.

'What do you mean?' he demanded, and had hardly spoken when a spine-chilling, bloodcurdling howl came from the other side of the door. They both jumped and stiffened in shocked surprise.

'Whatever was that?' breathed Kate.

'Padraic,' said Sean, rolling away from her and off the

bed. 'I'd forgotten about him. He wants to be let out and if I don't attend to him he'll make a mess and then Agnes will be after me.' The dog howled mournfully again and Sean called through the door, 'Okay, boy, I'll be with you in a minute.' Going across to the chair where he had put his clothes, he began to slip off his pyjama trousers.

Kate looked the other way, but inexorably her glance slid back against her will and she watched shamelessly as he dressed, noting how much thinner he was, how the ribs and collarbones showed through his skin, which was much paler than it had been in Mexico. He was too thin and too pale. He looked as if he had been very ill, in the way she had been in San Marco after the plane crash.

'What's wrong with your leg?' she asked abruptly, watching him move towards the door. 'Why are you limping?'

With a hand on the doorknob he turned to give her one of his cool noncommittal glances.

'And there was me thinking it didn't show too much these days,' he said. 'I was in an accident.'

'Where? Abroad?'

'No. Here, in Ireland.'

'When?'

'What's it to you?' he jeered.

'I'd like to know.'

'Why?'

'Because . . . because . . .' She broke off as the dog howled plaintively again and scratched at the door. 'Oh, if you don't want to tell me, it doesn't matter,' she muttered, flouncing over on her side and presenting her back to him.

The dog howled again. The door opened. Sean said, 'Okay, boy, we'll go for a walk.' The door closed and there was silence.

Kate sighed and stared at the pattern of roses on the wallpaper. He must have been badly hurt to have been left with a limp like that, yet she hadn't been informed. Why not? Didn't Irish authorities inform next of kin? But then perhaps Sean didn't acknowledge her as his next of kin. Perhaps he didn't think of her as his wife.

With another sigh she rolled over on to her other side. She still felt dopey from the drink he had given her last night. Another couple of hours' sleep would do wonders for the cold, and then, after talking to Sean and asking him to agree to a divorce by consent, she would go on her way. She would go to Dublin, find Hugh and ask him why he had played such a trick on her by inviting her to come here, all the time knowing that Sean was here.

When she woke up again it was almost noon and the room was full of bright sunshine. Her head felt lighter and she could breathe more easily. Getting out of bed, she went over to the window and looked out.

Rough green fields, criss-crossed with stone walls, sloped down to a crescent of yellow sand curving between two rocky headlands. Scattered across the emerald grass which topped the headlands, white sheep grazed peacefully. Little waves edged with lacy white foam tumbled on the sand, rolling in from a wide expanse of unbelievably blue ocean on which small rocky islands seemed to be floating.

Kate lingered for a while absorbing the tranquillity of the scene, amazed by the clarity of the visibility after the previous day's rain. Pushing open the window, she leaned out to look into the cobbled yard, expecting to see the red car. It wasn't there, and yet she had parked it directly opposite the front door, so she would be able to see it from this window. Where was it? Had Sean managed to get it going and moved it?

She closed the window and looked around for her clothes, then remembered that Sean had taken them from the bathroom down to the kitchen to dry. She would have to wear something else. But where had he put her suitcase? It didn't seem to be in the room. Only her dressing gown was there, draped over a chair. Under the chair were her moccasin-styled leather shoes.

Pulling on the dressing gown and slipping on the shoes, she went along to the bathroom. While she washed she examined herself critically in the mirror, remembering how she had looked when she had first met Sean. Well, in spite of having a red nose because of a cold, she looked much better than the skinny, big-eyed waif he had married. She looked much more like the photograph he had carried in his diary. Did he still possess that photograph? she wondered.

Downstairs there was no one in the lounge, but it was neat and tidy and the fireplace had been cleaned out and a new fire set. Hearing sounds coming from the kitchen, Kate walked towards it and pushed open the door, startling the grey-haired woman who was standing at the table holding a large mixing bowl in the crook of her arm while she whipped a creamy foam with rapid turns of a wooden spoon.

'Mother of God, what a fright you were after giving me!' exclaimed the woman. 'And who the divil are you?'

CHAPTER FIVE

As surprised to see the woman as the woman was to see her, Kate blurted,

'I'm Kate Lawson. Who are you?'

'Agnes Daley. And what might you be doing here?' demanded the woman. Tall, broad-shouldered and broad-bosomed, she was wearing a pink blouse which clashed rather violently with a bright red flannel skirt which had once been the traditional wear of women throughout the western part of Ireland. Her greying dark hair was looped back into a tight knot at the nape of her neck and her round eyes were a watery bluish-grey. Their glance was very disapproving as it took in Kate's dressing gown.

'Didn't Uncle Hugh . . . I mean Mr O'Connor tell you I would be coming?' asked Kate, advancing into the room. 'I'm his niece.'

'Now why should he be telling me anything about you?' replied Agnes. She set the mixing bowl down on the table and began to grease a baking tin.

'He invited me to come and stay here. I wrote to him telling him that I'd be arriving yesterday, but he can't have received my letter yet.'

'Sure and there was a letter came for him the other day. Mr Kierly readdressed it and sent it on to Dublin,' replied Agnes. 'But I'm wondering what right Mr O'Connor thought he had to be inviting anyone to come and stay in this house.' She gave Kate a fierce suspicious stare. 'He was only a guest here himself for a few days a couple of weeks ago.'

'A guest? But I thought . . .' Kate groped for a kitchen chair, pulled it out from under the table and sat down on it. 'Would you mind telling me who owns this house. Is it yours?'

'It is not. It belongs to Mr Sean Kierly. His grandfather Mr James Kierly left it to him in his will when he died, God rest his soul. I'm just the housekeeper here. I come every morning to clean up, do a bit of baking and washing if there's any to do. I did it for Mrs James Kierly and ever since Mr Sean came here six weeks ago I've been doing it for him,' Agnes replied, and began to scoop the creamy mixture out of the bowl and to drop it in great dollops into the cake tin. 'Are you sure now that Mr O'Connor didn't tell you that when he invited you to come here?'

'Quite sure,' said Kate between her teeth, realising how Hugh had tricked her. Agnes gave her another assessing suspicious glance, then picking up the cake tin went over to the oven, which was the old-fashioned sort built next to the fire which was burning slowly in the grate. She opened the oven door and the smell of pies baking wafted into the room, making Kate's mouth water.

'So you're Mr O'Connor's niece,' said Agnes as she removed two pies from the oven and put the cake in it. Closing the oven door, she carried the pies over to the table and put them on an asbestos sheet to cool. 'I'm thinking Mr Kierly would be surprised when you arrived. He wouldn't have been expecting you. If he'd known you were coming he'd have told me.'

'I suppose so,' muttered Kate. She was still feeling angry with her uncle for having placed her in such an embarrassing position. 'Didn't he tell you I was here when you saw him this morning?'

'He'd gone out before I came.' Agnes began to pick up the utensils she had used for making the pies and the cake and carried them over to the sink under the window. 'How did you get here?' she asked.

'I drove here,' said Kate. Agnes gave her a highly sceptical glance over one shoulder as she swished water noisily about in the sink. 'I did, really. I parked the car outside the front door. It wouldn't start last night, there was something wrong with the battery, and that's why Mr Kierly insisted that I stay even though my uncle wasn't here. It's a red Mini, but it isn't where I left it. Have you seen it?'

'I have not.' Agnes piled the dishes she had washed on the draining board, wiped her hands on a towel and opening a drawer in the table took out an embroidered Irish linen tablecloth. She spread it over one end of the table and began to set a place on it. 'There was no car in front of the house when I came this morning,' she said, and gave Kate another suspicious glance.

'Is there anywhere it could have been put by Mr Kierly?' asked Kate. 'Is there a garage?'

'Sure there is. It used to be the old barn. You could be looking in there, I suppose,' said Agnes, going over to a cupboard where food was stored.

'I'll take my clothes off the rack, then,' said Kate, and went to the cleat on the wall by the fireplace around which the rope holding the old-fashioned clothes rack was wound. She unwound it and let down the rack. Taking her clothes off it, she pulled the rack up again. 'You haven't seen my suitcase, I suppose?' she asked. 'It's a brown one. It isn't in the bedroom where I slept.'

'No, I have not,' said Agnes in her abrupt way, laying rashers of bacon in a frying pan. But you could be looking in the parlour for it and when you're dressed I'll have some breakfast ready for you.'

'Thank you.'

Relieved that Agnes seemed to be growing less suspicious of her, Kate left the kitchen and went into the lounge, but although she looked in every corner and behind every piece of furniture she found nothing belonging to her.

In the bedroom she dressed quickly in the tweed skirt and silky striped blouse she had worn the previous day and automatically looked around for her handbag. The last time she remembered having it she had been in the car. Had she left it on the front seat? With a sigh of exasperation she picked up the man's hairbrush which was lying on the dressing table and brushed the tangles out of her hair, leaving it hanging loose about her shoulders.

Where had Sean put her suitcase after he had taken her dressing gown and nightdress out of it? She opened the wardrobe door. Clothes belonging to Sean hung in it, a suit of dark grey finely worsted wool, some pairs of casual trousers, a suede jacket and a tweed jacket. But there was no brown suitcase and none of her clothes hanging in the wardrobe. The suitcase wasn't under the bed either.

Perhaps he had put it in one of the other rooms. She left the bedroom and went into the room next to it. Small, neatly furnished with a single bed, dressing table and wardrobe, it had an unused feel to it. So had the other small room across the landing. Her suitcase was in neither of them.

The smell of bacon cooking made her realise how hungry she was and giving up the search for the time being she went downstairs. Sunlight shafted in through the glass fanlight over the front door and glinted on the mirror on the hallstand. The tweed hat which she thought belonged to Hugh had gone and so had the fishing rod which had been propped up against the stand.

On impulse Kate opened the front door and looked outside. Warm yellow sunshine, air smelling of salt and seaweed, the sound of waves falling on the little beach and the cry of seagulls greeted her. The cobbled yard was empty.

Going down the steps, she walked round the side of the house to the whitewashed building which had once been a barn. The doors were closed. Kate pulled one of them open and peered inside. In the dimness she could see only an old cart which had once been pulled by a horse or a donkey. There was no red Mini and no room for one beside the cart, either.

Frowning, realising she couldn't leave unless she had her handbag, her suitcase and the car, Kate wandered back to the house. In the kitchen Agnes placed a plate of bacon and eggs on the table and began to pour tea into willow-patterned blue and white cups which were almost as big as dishes.

'Did you find your case?' she asked as Kate sat down and picked up the knife and fork.

'No. Nor my handbag. And the car isn't in the barn. It's as if everything had been spirited away.' Kate laughed a little, remembering the stories which her mother had told her about the 'wee folk', a band of mysterious super-natural people given to playing mischievous tricks who were supposed to have inhabited Ireland at one time. 'Perhaps the little people have been around,' she added teasingly.

'Now, never be saying that,' Agnes chided seriously, and crossed herself superstitiously. She sat down at the table and drew the cup of tea towards her. 'I'm thinking that perhaps Mr Kierly got your car started and took it into the village so that Martin McCormic can have a look at it. He's a good mechanic, is Martin. There isn't anything he can't make work.'

'Perhaps he did, but that doesn't explain where my suitcase is. My handbag could be still in the car, but not the suitcase. He brought the case into the house last night. I know he did because he . . .' Kate paused and gave Agnes a wary glance. It wouldn't do to tell the woman such an intimate detail. She would likely be shocked at the know-ledge that Mr Kierly had taken nightclothes out of the case of a young woman who was not, apparently, related to him. 'I know he did because I took my nightclothes out of it.'

'It's puzzling, for sure,' said Agnes with a nod. 'And you'll just have to wait until he comes back and ask him where he's put it.'

'I suppose I will,' said Kate. She was beginning to think that she was the victim not only of her uncle's trickery but also of Sean's mischief. He had hidden the case and the car so that she couldn't leave while he was out. But why? What did he hope to gain by delaying her?

'How long were you housekeeper to Mr James Kierly?' she asked Agnes.

'For over twenty years, ever since he bought this house. He claimed it had belonged to the Kierly family, long ago, before the family emigrated to America. He was a fine old gentleman, so he was. He wanted to spend the last part of his life here, he said, in the land of his forefathers, and while he was living here he wrote his memoirs. A most interesting life he had led as a journalist in the States. You wouldn't believe the famous people he'd known. He finished the book a few weeks before he died. Mr Sean was taking it to London to a publisher there when he had that accident.' Agnes took a noisy sip of tea. 'My God,' she muttered, 'and what a terrible thing that was, to be sure!' She shook her head slowly from side to side.

'What happened?'

'The car he was driving skidded on a wet road and slid sideways into a lorry which was coming the other way. He was lucky to survive. He was in hospital over six months, getting his leg fixed and learning to walk again. He came here to convalesce.'

'When did the accident happen?' Kate asked, doing some rapid mental arithmetic. Sean had been here six weeks and had been in the hospital over six months.

'Just before Christmas, on the way to Dun Laoghaire. He was going to catch the ferry to Holyhead. He broke his leg in two places and cracked some ribs. I believe he had concussion too, and I daresay you know what queer effects that has on a person.'

'Yes, I know,' said Kate. Had Sean suffered from temporary loss of memory as she had?

'And he's not right yet,' stated Agnes vehemently. 'Give him his due, your uncle, Mr O'Connor, was very concerned about him while he was staying here. He told me he didn't think it was good for Mr Sean to be living alone here. I heard them arguing about it a few times.' Agnes finished drinking her tea and stood up. 'Well, I must get on with me work. I have the beds to make. Which room did you sleep in, miss? I hope the bed was aired enough. Did Mr Sean find some sheets for you?'

'Er . . . I . . . yes.' Kate stood up hurriedly. What would Agnes think if she found out only one bed had been slept in? 'I'll make the beds for you,' she said.

'Now, that's good of you,' said Agnes. 'And I'll leave dusting the rooms until tomorrow morning, then. Just now I'll wash up these dishes while the cake is baking. I like to be away by one o'clock to attend to my own house.'

'Where do you live?' asked Kate.

'In the village of Dunane, at the top of the river estuary. It's a half mile walk from here. Have you ever heard of Dunane Castle?'

'No, I haven't. I haven't been to this part of Ireland before. Is the castle famous?'

'They say it dates from the first century A.D. and that there used to be a fort or dun there. Thomas Cavanagh owns the castle now and it's been turned into a tourist attraction. Miss Nuala Cavanagh is the hostess there this summer. She's an actress and sometimes appears on the stage in Dublin. She's been in a couple of films too. You'll have heard of her, perhaps?'

'I'm afraid not,' said Kate.

'She and Mr Sean are close friends. She brought him out here from the hospital and came over to see me to ask me to keep house for him while he stays here. She comes most days to visit him. She's a lovely lass, bright and cheery, and I wouldn't be at all surprised if they get married one of these days, when Mr Sean has stopped gallivanting off to those foreign parts. It's time he settled down and raised a family, so it is. There won't be any Kierlys left if he doesn't.'

Nuala Cavanagh: Kate said the name to herself as she went upstairs. The name of a woman Sean might marry one day. But how could he marry anyone when he was married to her? The strange sharp feeling which she had experienced the night before when he had mentioned that he had gone to a party with a woman in Dublin and then had taken her home afterwards twisted through her. He had been with that woman instead of going to England to visit her. Then he had been in an accident and the woman had brought him here to convalesce, behaving as if she had every right to look after him.

She wasn't jealous, she assured herself quickly, as she began to make the bed. How could she be jealous? She wasn't in love with Sean any more. Her love for him hadn't survived separation from him nor the casual way in which he had treated her. If it had survived she would have responded to him this morning in this bed. She would have made love with him.

The bed made, she wandered over to the window. Sunlight danced dazzlingly on the sea. She should go out and walk. The fresh air would blow away the remnants of her cold and by the time she came back to the house Sean might be here with the car. Picking up her cardigan, she slung it round her shoulders, went downstairs and let herself out through the front door.

Behind the barn there was a path which wound between a tangle of hawthorn, over which honeysuckle and bindweed straggled. It led to the banks of a small stream. Beyond the stream the land rose in low curves of purple heather, swelling up to the rounded top of a hill. Among the heather patches of black peat seemed to swallow the sunlight and in hollows feathery white bog cotton clung to straight reedy stalks. Higher up the hill the golden whin bushes blazed and overhead the high piping of a lark was raised above the brooding quiet of the countryside.

Walking beside the stream, Kate ducked under low branches of willows and trod on moss-covered rocks. The stream widened into a pool where more willows overhung a sheer rocky bluff. A slow current made a ripple on the smooth darkness of the pool.

Sean was standing on a gravelly spit which ran out almost to the middle of the pool. His trousers covered by high thigh waders, his Aran sweater gleaming softly in the sunlight, the brown tweed hat aslant on his head, he cast his line and laid the fly on the end of it dangerously close to the trailing branches of a willow on the other side, and the current carried it to the edge of a quiet dark backwater.

Finding a convenient flat-topped rock, Kate sat down and watched. The point of Sean's rod jerked. Did that mean he had a bite? He struck downwards with the rod. It quivered and seemed to curve into a half circle. A fin came up out of the water and threshed under it again. For the next few seconds the quiet place was noisy with the sounds of threshing water as the fish leapt about trying to free itself. Then suddenly the fight was over and Sean was coming towards the bank, rod held high, the glittering fish still jumping, hanging from the hook. He saw her at once.

'How would you like trout for your supper tonight?' he asked, and leaning beside the rock he began to take the hook out of the fish's mouth.

'There isn't much on that for two,' Kate said critically.

'I have more,' he said, and lifting a canvas satchel from the ground showed her the other three trout he had caught. 'It's been a good morning.'

'You'll have to eat them all yourself,' she said coolly. 'I won't be here for supper.'

'Where will you be?'

'On my way to Dublin.'

'How will you get there?'

'The same way I came, in the car. I rented it at the airport and I have to return it there. Where is it? What have you done with it?'

'I tried to start it again this morning, but no dice, so I phoned Martin McCormic in Dunane and he came out to look at it. He said the electrics were damp too and it would take a while to dry out. He towed it away to his garage,' he replied.

'You should have told me,' Kate objected.

'You were fast asleep,' he retorted smoothly.

'How long is a while?'

'A day or two, Martin said.'

'Oh, that's ridiculous!' she protested. 'I must have it this afternoon.'

'No one works fast in this part of the world,' Sean drawled. 'And when you come to live here you have to throw away your watch. Nothing you say will make Martin hurry if he doesn't want to. You'll not be leaving this afternoon.'

'But . . . but I can't stay! I have to be back in Westcourt the day after tomorrow. I have an appointment to keep.'

'Too bad,' he mocked.'

Kate glanced at him uneasily, but he wasn't looking at her. He was too intent on doing something to his fishing rod.

'Agnes Daley told me Moyvalla House belongs to you,' she said.

'I bet she was surprised to find a strange woman in the house,' he said with a laugh.

'No more surprised than I was to learn from her that Uncle Hugh isn't the owner,' she retorted. 'Why didn't you tell me you'd inherited the house from your grandfather?'

'I didn't get much of a chance to tell you,' he replied dryly. 'What else did Agnes tell you?'

'She told me how badly you were hurt in that accident. She said you were on your way to catch the ferry to Holyhead when it happened. Were you?'

'That's right. It was after I'd taken Nuala back to her flat after the party. I guess I'd cut things a bit fine and was driving too fast for the state of the road. 'I was going to see a publisher in London.' He paused, then added in a low voice, 'And then I was going to see you, as you know, because I sent you a card to tell you I'd be coming. I was going to tell you all this last night, only you wouldn't listen.'

'I'm sorry,' she muttered. 'I wish I'd known you'd been hurt. I should have been told. Why wasn't I told?'

Sean propped his rod against a nearby tree and came back to stand in front of her. Crossing his arms across his chest, he stared at her frowningly.

'I thought you had been told,' he said.

'No. And when you didn't come and I didn't hear from you I thought you must have changed your mind and decided you didn't want to see me after all,' she whispered.

'As soon as I was well enough to know what was going on I asked someone to tell you.'

'Someone?' she queried, looking up.

'A friend—at least someone whom I thought was a friend.' His mouth twisted cynically and he pushed his hat to the back of his head. 'Oh, well, it doesn't matter now.

The damage has been done,' he added sardonically.

'Even Hugh didn't tell me,' she complained.

'Hugh didn't know about the accident until he came here a few weeks ago. He didn't even know I was living here until he started making enquiries about me. I guess he did that after he'd received your letter.'

'Did he tell you I'd asked him if he knew where you were?'

'No. He did talk about you, though, said how proud he was of your achievements and how you were enjoying your career as a teacher. I got the impression from him that you were getting along fine.

Kate stared at the pool. In the shadow of the willows the water was blackish brown, but in the sunlight it glimmered with gold and olive lights. Her glance lifted to the high brownish crown of the hill. In the sky white clouds were sailing and somewhere a bird kept up a monotonous piping tune. It was a lovely tranquil place, so different from the other places in which she had been with Sean, so different from the dry desert heat of San Marco, the sharp brittle cold of San Cristobal and the torrid steaminess of Tuxtla. It was a pleasant green place where nobody hurried, a place where she could stay and get to know Sean better. And yet she couldn't stay.

'Did you tell Agnes about our . . . our relationship?' asked Sean.

'No. When she asked me who I was I gave her my maiden name through force of habit.' She turned to him to explain, met the cool gaze of grey eyes and looked away again. 'I . . . I've never used the name Kierly and I've never told anyone we were married in San Marco.'

'Until you met Barry Wyman,' he suggested tersely.

'Yes, I told Barry.' She flicked him another quick glance, to see him still watching her coldly. 'It . . . it just came out when he asked me to marry him,' she added defensively.

'How long have you known him?'

'Since last November. He came to Netherfield, the school where I teach, to hear his daughter perform in a concert.'

'Widowed or divorced?'

'He divorced his wife some years ago. I've seen him several times since we first met, but I'd no idea he was thinking of marriage until a few weeks ago.'

More silence between them. Kate's glance flicked to Sean, then back to the pool. The water tinkled against rocks and in the trees birds whistled and piped. Grasses rustled as a breeze ruffled them and the tops of the trees shimmered with reflected light.

'Slept with him yet?'

The laconic, casually drawled question stung her like the flick of a whip and she rounded on him. Between their dark lashes his eyes glittered icily and there was an unpleasant curl to his upper lip.

'You have no right to ask a question like that!' she spat out at him.

'No?' he jeered. 'But some people, the priest who married us for instance, might say I have every right, since you're still my wife.' There was another strained silence before he added gruffly, 'I can't understand why you didn't do what I suggested. Why didn't you go to a lawyer and arrange to have the marriage dissolved as soon as you got back to England? It would have been so simple. Or you could have had it done any time during the past two years, while I've been abroad. Why haven't you done anything about it before now?' He sounded angry, almost as if he felt she had let him down by not dissolving the marriage.

It hurt to know that he felt like that, and the pool blurred before her eyes, became an abstract shape of glinting green, yellow and brown light.

'Why haven't you?' she countered, and her voice shook uncontrollably.

'Ha!' His short laugh was bitter. 'A good question. For many reasons, the chief one being that I've been busy trying to stay alive, not only in San Marco but also in some other troubled places in the world. I was in prison for six weeks in one country, for instance.'

'Why?' She stared at him in amazement.

'For reporting the truth, that's all. For making sure the world knew there were two sides to the situation.' He paused, drew a deep breath and added more quietly, 'I expected you to do something about our marriage . . . if you wanted to.'

Supposing she said to him now, *I didn't want to because I hoped it would turn out differently and develop into a real marriage*, what would he say? He would jeer at her, probably, accuse her of being sentimental and romantic, and she couldn't risk that. She didn't want to be hurt any more by him.

She looked at him again. He was watching her, but his eyes were no longer cold. Their expression was blatantly sensual as they studied her face, then her throat, the deep V of her blouse which just showed the cleft between her breasts, and came back to her mouth and up to meet her eyes. His long-lipped mouth softened into the tantalising white smile which made her catch her breath.

'You've filled out a little since the last time I saw you. No bones showing through now,' he said. Stepping towards her, he touched her cheek with his fingertips. 'Soft yet firm, like a peach, good enough to eat,' he said softly. His finger-tips spread out over her cheek, cool against the sunwarmed skin, sending icy tingles through her. They slid up and lifted a swathe of her hair away from her head. 'It glows like fire,' he murmured, and wound the thick strand around his hand, holding her captive. The tiny yellowish flecks flared smokily in his eyes as he looked deeply into her eyes, mesmerising her so that she swayed involuntarily towards him, her breasts brushing against his chest, her lips parting as they anticipated the touch of his.

'There've been times lately when I believed I'd never see you again, but now that I have, now that you're here, I'd like you to stay a while, Kate,' he said persuasively.

'I . . . I . . . can't stay,' she whispered breathlessly, closing her ears to the voice inside her which was shouting out wildly, *I want to stay. I'm going to stay.* 'I must leave for Dublin this afternoon.'

'I'm not going to let you,' he murmured, bending his head coming so close to her that she had only a foreshortened view of his face; of the sharp angle of a cheekbone, the silky thickness of black lashes around a yellowish-grey eye. Then the warmth of his lips was against hers, seducing them with gentleness, tormenting them with a promise of passion before he raised his head to look down at her again and whisper, 'Please stay, Kate, for a few days . . . and nights.'

'No.' She pulled her hair from his grasp and standing up, backed away from him. 'I can't stay. I have to go back to England. I must be there on September the first, the day after tomorrow.'

'So you could stay one more night,' he argued. 'You could leave tomorrow and still be in England the day afterwards.'

'No. I can't stay another night here . . . with you.'

'Why not?' His mouth took on a hard line.

'Because . . . oh, because I think you only want me to stay because I'm a woman,' she blurted.

One corner of his mouth quirked and a dark eyebrow flickered with sardonic amusement, but the expression in his eyes didn't change. If anything they grew more sultry.

'I admit that has a lot to do with the way I'm feeling,' he agreed. 'Seeing you again, lying in bed with you last night and this morning, has awakened appetites I was beginning to believe had been destroyed by that accident.' He stepped towards her again, his glance centring provocatively on her mouth. 'Remember the night in San Cristobal, Kate, and how you felt then?' he asked softly. 'I guess I'm going through a similar experience. I'm suddenly glad to be alive and I feel as if I'm on fire here.' He struck his fist against his stomach.

'Then any woman would do,' she retorted, backing away from him. 'But I'm not available, and what you're feeling has nothing to do with me being who I am. It has nothing to do with you loving me or with us being married.' Her voice shook with the violence of lacerated emotions. 'I told you this morning I don't want to make love with you. It wouldn't mean anything to me. I . . . I . . . was in love with you in San Cristobal, otherwise I wouldn't have asked you to make love to me. But I'm not in love with you any more. What you predicted in Tuxtla has happened—what I felt for you then has faded away, so I can't stay with you tonight or longer. Now will you please be sensible and tell me where my case and handbag are so I can leave and walk to the village?'

The small amount of colour in Sean's face drained away. The skin was suddenly chalk-white so that the dark stubble of his beard, his lashes and brows, his hair looked jet black in contrast and the hollows beneath his eyes caused by illness seemed deeper. Muscles ridged along his jaw as he struggled for control and the warmth faded from his eyes, leaving them cold and sharp. She had the strangest feeling as he stared at her that he could see right into her mind and observe the confusion which was raging there.

'Okay, you win,' he drawled with a shrug, turning away from her to take hold of his fishing rod. 'If you don't want to stay you don't want to stay. You'll find your case and handbag in a cupboard on the landing between the bathroom and my bedroom.'

'Thank you.' She should be feeling pleased she had won, but instead she was feeling the awful dragging let down of anti-climax. 'Sean, I . . .'

'If you're going to say you're sorry, forget it,' he snarled, swinging round on her. 'Go back to the house, get your things and clear out—the sooner the better.'

'All right, I will,' she retorted stiffly.

She set off down the path as fast as she could, trying to pretend she wasn't disappointed because he had let her go so easily. But why be disappointed? What had she hoped he would do? Had she hoped he would play the caveman and force her to stay and sleep with him? She would have hated him for ever if he had done that. She hated him now because he had confused her and she couldn't see her way clearly any more.

Dreaming in the warm sunshine, its white walls glowing against the vivid green land, the house came into view. Beyond it the moving ocean flashed blue and silver. Among the golden-white flowers of the honeysuckle which spangled the unkempt hedges edging the pathway bees hummed busily and on the unseen sandy shore the little waves sighed softly.

It wouldn't do to stay too long in this place anyway, thought Kate, as she went up the steps to the front door. It would capture you if you did. As she opened the door sunlight slanted in across the dark floor of the hall and she remembered reading a story somewhere about the people who lived in the west of Ireland and how they could tell the time of day by the slant of the sun coming in through their open doorways. Using the doors as sundials, they had had no need of clocks.

But there was a clock at Moyvalla and sunlight glinted on its gilt fingers where they pointed to twenty past two. Agnes had long since left and the house was quiet. The stairs creaked as Kate went up them. She would get her case and handbag and walk to Dunane. Half a mile, Agnes had told her. When she got there she would insist that Martin McCormic make her car roadworthy immediately. By five o'clock she should be on her way to Ennis where she would stay the night. Tomorrow she would reach Dublin in the afternoon. By nightfall she would be in Westcourt.

She went straight to the cupboard wondering why she hadn't noticed it when she had been searching for her things earlier. Her hand closed confidently round the doorknob. She turned it and pulled, but the door remained closed. She pulled again. Nothing happened. The door was locked and there was no key in the lock.

CHAPTER SIX

REFUSING to believe that the door was locked, thinking that perhaps it was merely stuck with dampness, Kate tugged and tugged at the doorknob. The door remained obstinately shut and didn't even shake when she kicked it to give vent to her anger. Sean had tricked her. He had been quite willing to tell her where he had put her case and handbag because he had known she could not get into the cupboard.

From below came the sound of Sean entering the house. Coming through the hall, he talked to the setter. The lounge door creaked as he pushed it open, creaked again as he swung behind him to close it. But it didn't close.

It seemed he wasn't interested in finding out whether Kate had opened the cupboard door or not. He was going to take his ease in the lounge and wait for her to react. Well, she wasn't going down yet. There must be some way to get the door of the cupboard open without appealing for his help.

Still seething inwardly with anger because he had deceived her, Kate went into the bedroom and searched the top of the dressing table and chest of drawers for a key. There was none. But there was a key in the bedroom door. Would it fit the cupboard lock? She took it out and went back to the cupboard, but although the key slid into the lock it would not turn.

She tried the keys she found in the other doors too, but none of them opened the cupboard. Returning to the bedroom where she had slept, she stared out of the window. She supposed she could go without her case, but she wouldn't get very far without her handbag because she would need money to pay for the repairs to the car, buy petrol and pay the rental agency what extra she owed for the hire of the car. She would need money to pay for a night's lodgings.

How could she persuade Sean to open the cupboard for her? Against her hot forehead the glass of the window was cool and once again the tranquillity of the scene before her soothed her mind. She wished she could stay in this quiet house with Sean. The green fields, the web of grey stone walls, the pale sand of the beach, the blue of the sea all ran into one another like a painting that has been smudged as she recalled what he had said beside the pool. He wanted her and if she stayed he would make love to her. If only he had said he loved her she might, she just might have agreed to stay. . . .

Her thoughts came spinning to a stop as the sound of a

car's engine shattered the warm silence of the afternoon. Everything became distinct again and Kate straightened up in anticipation, sure she would see the red car appear round the corner of the house. But the car which came into sight was a black Volkswagen. It stopped in front of the house and a woman got out of it. She was tall and had long straight black hair. She walked round the car towards the house and disappeared.

The front door bell tinkled and was answered by Padraic's sharp bark. Kate left the bedroom and lingered on the landing, listening to Sean's footsteps as he went to the front door. She heard the door open, then the lilt of the woman's voice as she spoke. The front door was closed and the same voice became a murmur as the woman went with Sean into the lounge.

Who was the woman? Nuala Cavanagh? Who else? Her curiosity tinged with jealousy, Kate went back into the bedroom and tidied her hair quickly. She would go down now to the lounge and ask Sean for the key to the cupboard while the woman was there. He could hardly refuse to give it to her in front of Nuala. And when Nuala left Kate would leave with her.

In the lounge the woman was gracefully draped in a corner of the couch, talking to Sean over the back of it. He was leaning against the wall beside the rosewood cabinet, a glass in his hand. Kate went right up to him, ignoring the other woman.

'The cupboard door is locked,' she said, cutting across the melodious drone of the woman's voice. 'Please may I have the key?' She held out her hand to him, all the time looking at him directly.

'Lord love us, Sean, why didn't you tell me you have company?' exclaimed Nuala Cavanagh, speaking with a slight yet attractive Irish brogue.

Sean emptied his glass and turned to the cabinet to pour

more whiskey. Glass in his hand again, he turned to face Kate. There were patches of high colour on his cheekbones and his eyes glittered unpleasantly.

'I haven't got the key,' he said clearly and slowly, and drank some whiskey.

'Sean, aren't you going to introduce us?' The woman's voice was gently rebuking, as if she were speaking to a bad-mannered youth.

'Kate, this is Nuala Cavanagh. Nuala, meet Kate,' Sean growled, ungraciously waving his glass first towards one of them and then towards the other before tilting it again to his mouth.

Kate turned and nodded politely at Nuala. The woman was much as she had imagined her to be, a stately Irish beauty with a low broad forehead, deep-set vivid blue eyes, high rounded cheekbones, a wide full-lipped mouth, a strong square jaw and a nose that turned downwards. Her complexion was delicately pink and white, accentuated by the inky blackness of her thick coarse hair and strongly marked eyebrows.

'Kate?' Nuala murmured wonderingly in her deep rich voice, and her eyes widened enquiringly.

'San Marco,' said Sean laconically, and poured more whiskey.

'Oh, that Kate?' Nuala's white neck arched back as she laughed gaily, showing big straight teeth. 'Forgive my amusement,' she added, speaking to Kate in a friendly fashion, 'but Sean told me about the adventure you and he had together in San Marco. He told me you had to go through some form of marriage ceremony with him before you were allowed to leave the country.'

'Not a form of marriage,' said Sean slowly, as if he were having difficulty in enunciating his words. 'It was the real thing, before a Catholic priest, just as it would be done in this country. Holy Matrimony which no man ... or woman either . . . shall put asunder.'

'I realise that,' said Nuala with a touch of impatience and giving him a wary rather vindictive glance. 'But you've never lived together properly, have you, like husband and wife? It was a marriage of expedience.' She looked at Kate again and smiled. 'I don't suppose you had any difficulty in having it dissolved when you got back to England, did you? Divorce is so easy to get there these days.'

'I . . . it . . . we aren't divorced yet,' muttered Kate, and the beautiful blue eyes narrowed in puzzlement.

'I see. So what brings you to this part of the world?' asked Nuala.

'I was at the music festival at Ennis and being near here I thought I'd call in yesterday. I wouldn't be here now, only there's something wrong with my car and . . .'

'It's at McCormic's,' Sean interrupted her. 'Martin says it will take him a couple of days to fix it, so Kate's staying until it's ready.' He sounded very aggressive and Kate turned to him, ready to disagree. Over the rim of his glass his eyes met hers arrogantly.

'If you're really interested in Irish ballads and folk songs you should come to the castle while you're here and see the pageant,' said Nuala pleasantly before Kate could speak. 'We have a great group of folk singers performing there. You may have heard of them. They're called the Green Folk.'

'Yes, I have, and I'd love to hear them,' said Kate, her wits working quickly. 'But how could I get there without a car?'

'I could drive you there, later,' said Nuala, getting to her feet. 'I'm on my way to Kilburke now. I called in here hoping Sean might come for the ride with me. I'll pick you up on the way back.' She glanced past Kate at Sean. 'You'll come this evening too, won't you, darling?' she added. 'You haven't seen me in the role of the medieval chatelaine of the castle yet.'

Sean set down his empty glass and pushed away from the wall.

'I've seen you perform plenty of other roles, so I think I'll give this one a miss,' he drawled unpleasantly. 'Excuse me, I've just remembered I haven't had any lunch yet.'

Nuala watched him leave the room. It seemed to Kate that the woman's mouth looked a little pinched, and she realised Nuala was much older than she appeared to be at first sight, possibly older than Sean.

'He isn't very well,' Nuala said abruptly. Her glance went to the empty glass and the whiskey bottle. 'But I've never known him drink too much in the afternoon before.' The blue eyes slid round and fixed accusingly on Kate's. 'Those of us who've been his friends for years have been very worried about him. You know about the accident, of course?'

'A little.'

'Before that happened he was always so active, loved his work as a foreign correspondent,' said Nuala. 'Now he can't move as fast as he could and that frustrates him, so he drinks too much and delays his recovery. And of course the news agency won't employ him again until he's fully recovered. It's become a vicious circle.' Nuala sighed heavily and surveyed Kate critically. 'And then you're somewhat to blame for the way he's feeling too.'

'Me?' exclaimed Kate. 'How?'

Nuala's wide expressive mouth twisted into a sad little smile and moving with long graceful strides, as if she were on the stage, she paced up and down the room, coming back to stand in front of Kate.

'I must tell you that Sean and I have known each other a

long time,' she said softly. 'We've confided our troubles to each other ever since we met here when James Kierly first brought him to Ireland. If we had been different people we would have married years ago. But both of us liked our freedom too much. I wanted to act; he wanted to be a reporter. So we decided some years ago that instead of getting married we would live together whenever it was possible; when we were both in the same place at the same time. Do you understand what I'm saying?'

'I think so,' said Kate stiffly, feeling as if she had just been kicked in the ribs. 'You and he are lovers.'

'We have been in the past. And we will be again, God willing,' whispered Nuala dramatically, her eyes veiled by their long lashes as she looked down at her hands that she was holding palms together, long fingers matching perfectly and pointing upwards close to her breast in an attitude of prayer that reminded Kate of the nuns at the Santa Rosa Mission.

'Last December he came to Dublin for the first time in three years,' Nuala intoned, her blue eyes flashing with emotion as she looked at Kate again. 'It was wonderful to meet again after so long a separation, but he refused to stay with me. He said he had to go to England, and it was then he told me about you and what had happened in San Marco.' Nuala looked down at her hands again. 'He said he had to find out if you'd done anything to dissolve the marriage. But he didn't reach England and since the accident he seems to have been too lethargic to go anywhere.' Nuala looked up again. 'I thought . . . I'm hoping you've come to see him to tell him what he and I both want to know,' she added. 'The marriage to you is on his mind, I know it is, torturing him, coming between him and me. He hates the idea of still being tied to you, of not being free. And I can see that you being here, with him in the same house, has upset him.'

'I wouldn't be here if . . . if . . . my uncle hadn't invited me to come,' Kate blurted defensively. 'I only wanted to know where Sean was so my lawyer could contact him and ask him to agree to a divorce by consent.'

'Oh, I'm glad, so very, very glad,' Nuala whispered. Her eyes were full of tears now and coming up to Kate she embraced her. 'It will make such a difference. I'm glad you came, Kate, and if there's anything I can do to help you . . .'

'You can help, by taking me to the castle this evening. I don't want to stay here another night with Sean. It . . . well, I'm sure you'll understand when I tell you he and I aren't comfortable in each other's company.'

'I understand,' said Nuala softly. 'And if your car isn't ready you can stay the night at the castle and welcome.' She looked at her watch. 'I must fly if I'm going to be at Kilburke by three-thirty. She walked to the door with a graceful swing of her hips and Kate followed her. 'I'll be back in about two hours,' she added. 'See you then.'

Alone in the lounge Kate waited until the front door had closed and she heard Nuala's car starting up. In two hours she would be leaving this house never to return, but first she had to get her suitcase and handbag from the cupboard. She looked down at her tweed skirt. She couldn't go to a banquet in a skirt and blouse—surely Sean would understand that?

In the kitchen he was sitting at the table. His head was resting on his hands, his elbows were on the table and he was reading a newspaper which he had spread open before him. Kate paused in the doorway, thinking over what Nuala had told her. That Sean was unhappy she didn't doubt, and perhaps Hugh had noticed too and that was why he had invited her to come here. But to what extent

Sean's unhappiness was due to his dislike of still being married to her, she couldn't be sure.

There was dejection in the slump of his shoulders that touched her heart suddenly, lighting in it a little flame of sympathy. The Sean she had known so briefly in San Marco and Mexico had been a cool, strong formidable man apparently invulnerable to hurt, and it was difficult for her to associate him with this other person who sometimes drank too much and seemed to have lost his zest for life.

The feeling of sympathy blazed up, urging her to go forward to put her arms about him and cradle his head against her breast as she remembered how compassionate he had been towards her when she had been in trouble in San Marco. She owed him some consideration, some gesture of kindness. Slowly she moved forward and was reaching out to touch his shoulder when he spoke abruptly without turning round.

'Has Nuala gone?'

Kate pulled up short in surprise. She hadn't realised he had known she was in the room.

'Yes. She said she'll come back at five-thirty to take me to the castle.' There were no signs of food on the table, no empty plates either. 'Have you had something to eat?' she asked.

'No.' The tersely spoken negative was discouraging.

'I'll make some sandwiches for you,' she said cheerfully, and crossed the room to the larder.

'Don't bother. I'll make something for myself later,' Sean said sharply.

'But . . .' She looked back at him. Head still between his hands, he was still staring at the paper.

'I said don't bother,' he repeated in the same sharp tones.

'I know you did, but I'm still going to make some sand-wiches for you. You shouldn't drink so much whiskey on an empty stomach. And you should eat regular meals. You'll get ulcers if you don't,' she retorted.

'So what?' He lifted his head to give her a vicious under-browed glare. 'Go away and leave me to go to the devil my own way. I didn't ask you to come here and inter-fere.'

'I'm not interfering!' she shot back at him, her temper flaring, and recalling what he had said to her the previous night when he had brought her the hot drink she added acidly, 'I'd do the same for anyone who was in need of food, and she went into the larder.

She made ham sandwiches from the fresh bread Agnes had left, boiled the kettle and made a mug of strong black instant coffee and placed them all before him on the table.

'There you are. That should help you to sober up,' she remarked caustically.

'I'm not drunk.' He gave her another hostile glare as she sat down opposite to him, but he reached out and picked up the mug of coffee.

'Well, you're not behaving normally, she countered.

'How do you know?' he jeered as he set the mug down after drinking from it and picked up a sandwich. 'How do you know what I'm like when I'm normal?'

Kate considered the question seriously while she watched him take a bite out of the sandwich and chew ravenously.

'If you were behaving normally you wouldn't be here,' she said at last. 'You'd be where the action is, in one of the places in the world where there's trouble, reporting on it instead of reading about it in a newspaper several days old.' He flicked a sharp glance at her from under frowning eyebrows, but said nothing. 'When you're well enough to go back to work will you go abroad again?' she asked.

'I don't know. It depends,' he replied noncommittally, and turned the page of the newspaper. Picking up another sandwich, he bit into it and went on reading or pretending to read as if determined to shut her out. She glanced at her watch. Almost twenty past four. Time she was changing her clothes and getting ready to go with Nuala—yet now, contrarily enough she didn't want to leave.

'Sean, I can hardly go to the banquet at the castle dressed like this,' she said.

He looked up and his glance roved over her curiously.

'Why not? What's wrong with your clothes? They look all right to me.'

'They're not suitable, and anyway I'd like to change my underwear too. Please will you give me the key to the cupboard.'

His eyes widened slightly and began to glint with mockery.

'Is it locked?' he queried on a lilt of surprise.

'Oh, you know it is.' She lost her cool suddenly. 'And I can't understand why you put my things in there and locked it in the first place.'

'I don't understand why I did either,' he replied. 'I must have been either drunk or crazy last night, thinking I could stop you from leaving. A little of both, perhaps. Could be I've gone crazy with living alone in this place, as Hugh said when he was here. I've gone nuts with brooding about that bloody accident, wondering why it happened and why it had to happen at that particular moment in time. . . .' His voice grated oddly, he broke off, swore and raked his fingers through his hair. 'But I don't suppose you're interested,' he added with a touch of weariness. 'Or worried. You should be, you know,' he went on tauntingly. 'You should be worried about my state of mind. You promised to love and comfort in sickness and in health.'

'So did you promise,' she retorted shakily, rising to her feet. 'But you didn't mean a word you said. If you had you wouldn't have stayed away from me all that time. And you would have written to me.'

'I told you at the time what being married to me would be like,' he replied tautly. 'And I seem to remember you said you wouldn't mind because you had a career to follow too.'

'Oh, what's the point in talking about it?' she whispered. 'It happened to two different people.'

'Did it?' Sean countered challengingly, and pushing to his feet picked up the empty coffee cup and went over to the stove to light the burner beneath the kettle. 'No,' he went on musingly, 'it happened to us, to you and to me, and now our past is catching up on us and we're having to do something about it.' Moving with a briskness which had been absent from his actions but which was familiar to Kate, he spooned coffee into the mug and poured boiling water on it. 'What would you like to do?' he asked, turning to face her, mug in his hand.

She stared at him, trying to guess what lay behind his change in manner. Bright between their dark lashes, his narrowed eyes returned her gaze as he sipped the hot coffee. She rubbed the palm of her hand nervously along the top rung of the ladderback chair on which she had been sitting, as she realised the moment of truth had arrived and there was no escape, no running away.

'As soon . . . as soon as I get back to England I'll tell my lawyer to contact you about arranging a divorce by consent.' She forced the word out between dry lips.

'So you can marry this Barry Wyman you talk about?' Sean queried coolly, and drank more coffee.

'So you can be free of me at last to live with Nuala?'

'Oh?' His eyebrows went up in satirical surprise. 'Now why would I want to do that?' he drawled, and drained the coffee mug.

'She's told me about the arrangement you and she made to live together whenever you're in the same place at the same time,' she explained. 'She said your marriage to me was coming between you and her. I wish I'd known about her before. I wish you'd told me about her at Tuxtla. I'd have understood then why you wanted the marriage dissolved so soon and I'd have done something about it right away. Now all I can do is ask you to agree to a divorce.'

'You and Nuala must have had a nice cosy chat once my back was turned,' he remarked acidly, turning away to set down the coffee mug. 'All right, tell your lawyer to write to me and we'll take it from there.'

Kate went limp and had to hold on to the chair back. It was done. She had asked him and he had more or less agreed.

'Could I have the key to the cupboard now?' she asked weakly.

'I haven't got it,' he replied, swinging round to face her again.

'Then tell me where it is.'

'I don't know where it is. I've lost it.'

'Lost it?' She was limp no longer. 'I don't believe you!' she raged. 'Oh, will you stop fooling about and give it to me or tell where it is.'

'I'm not fooling about,' he retorted. 'I'm telling the truth. I've lost the key to the cupboard.'

'Where? How? Sean, how could you be so careless? What did you do with it after you locked the cupboard?'

'I put it in my trouser pocket. This one, to be exact.' He pulled the lining out of the right pocket. 'You see, it's empty. It was empty this morning too, when I felt for the key.'

'Perhaps you took it out last night and put it somewhere else,' Kate suggested urgently, going up to him.

'I might not be perfectly normal, but I'm not so crazy I wouldn't remember,' he retorted dryly. 'I did not take it out of the pocket last night and put it somewhere else. I know because I've looked everywhere I can think of. I can only assume that I pulled it out of the pocket by accident when I took my handkerchief out last night while I was taking Padraic for his last walk. It's probably lying among the long grass on the hillside or even among the heather.'

'You've looked for it?'

'I've looked,' he returned shortly. 'It probably won't appear now until the winter, if then.'

'But I must have my handbag,' she whispered. 'It has money in it, my airline ticket, the keys for the flat, my cheque book, the letter accepting my application and telling me when to attend for the interview. . . .'

'What interview?' he demanded sharply.

'At the school where I work. It's for the day after tomorrow. I've applied for the position of head of the department of music—that's why I have to leave as soon as I can. I must get back in time for it.'

Sean stared down at her consideringly, almost suspiciously.

'Is this on the level?' he asked.

'Of course it is. Why would I lie about it? If . . . if you don't believe me I'll show you the letter I had from the headmistress once I have my handbag,' she said indignantly. 'Sean, you've got to open that cupboard!'

'Means a lot to you, that job, does it?' he queried. 'Means more to you than Barry Wyman?'

'Yes, it does. It means more to me than . . than any man,' she flared, glaring at him.

'Okay, point taken,' he said with a grin. 'I'll go and see if I can find a hacksaw to saw through the lock. If I can't find one . . . well, then I guess I'll just have to take a hatchet to the door.'

He found a hacksaw, but it seemed to take ages for him to saw through the steel lock. While he did it Kate leaned against the banisters which edged the landing and watched and they talked. She told him about the school and the small triumphs she had known during the year of teaching. He told her a little about the adventures he had had while covering the news in various trouble spots.

At last the lock broke in half and the door was opened. Kate took her case and handbag out.

'If you'd like to see the letter,' she said, beginning to open her handbag.

'No, I believe you,' he said brusquely, and went away down the stairs.

Going into the bathroom, she locked the door and began to strip off her clothing. Half an hour later she emerged wearing a dress of silky turquoise cotton patterned all over with tiny flowers in pink and white. Her hair was arranged in a smooth coil on top of her head and her face was delicately made up. In the bedroom she packed her dressing gown and nightgown, then gathering up her raincoat she made for the door.

There she paused and looked back, her thoughts winging back to the previous night and how Sean had looked after her. He could be very considerate when he chose to be. In fact it had been his consideration for her needs which had attracted her to him in San Marco and she had been deceived into thinking he cared deeply for her. Or she had let herself be deceived, she admonished herself warningly, turning away to go along the landing.

A car's horn tooted outside. Nuala was back. Kate hurried down the stairs and into the lounge. Sean wasn't there, nor was the red setter. Aware that Nuala was hooting the horn again impatiently, Kate went through to the kitchen. No Sean and no Padraic. It looked as if she would have to leave without saying goodbye after all.

When she opened the front door she was dazzled momentarily by the brilliance of the sunshine. As soon as she could see properly she went down the steps, realising that Sean was by the car talking to Nuala. There was no sign of the dog.

'Sorry to have kept you waiting, Nuala,' she said. 'Shall I put my case in the back seat?'

'No, put it in here,' opening the hood of the car. 'You'll have to sit in the back seat now that Sean is coming to the castle with us.'

Looking up from putting the case in the front of the car, Kate encountered Sean's cool unsmiling eyes. In the dark suit she had seen hanging in the closet in his room, with a crisp white shirt striped in blue and a dark red tie, his hair brushed tidily, he looked surprisingly suave and elegant, quite different from the suntanned, casually dressed man she had known in San Marco and even more different from the pale-faced, lethargic semi-invalid she had known for the past twenty-odd hours.

'I changed my mind,' he drawled in answer to her enquiring glance. 'I decided the time had come for me to see Nuala in her part in the pageant.' He turned to the car and pushed forward the front seat. 'Won't you get in?' he added politely.

The road to Dunane wandered about, sometimes dipping down close to the dimpling blue waters of a wide river estuary, sometimes curving between stone walls over which it was possible to see the land stretching away, shaded green, webbed by a tracery of stone walls and hedges, dotted by white farmhouses surrounded by clumps of trees.

They came to the village suddenly, round a sharp bend.

A few streets of white-walled single-storeyed houses with sharply pitched grey roofs, dominated by a grey stone church with a square tower, it had been built where the estuary narrowed into the river.

The road twisted down to the small harbour where, on the sun-bright water, *curraghs*, the traditional fishing boats of the west coast, made long dark shapes.

'Do you think we could go to the garage where my car is and find out if it's ready yet?' Kate asked, leaning forward to speak to Nuala.

'Martin won't be there at this time of the day. He'll have gone home for his tea,' said Sean coolly.

'Anyway, I haven't time to stop now,' said Nuala as she changed gear to turn the car over a hump-backed stone bridge which crossed the river. 'Don't worry. You can stay at the castle tonight and I'll bring you into the village first thing tomorrow morning.' Her black hair swirled on her shoulders as she turned her head to give Kate a bright warm smile.

'Thank you,' muttered Kate helplessly, giving up all hope of being able to leave and go on her way to Dublin that night.

Leaning back in her seat again, she looked out of the window. Sunlight glinted on the grey stone of battlements peeping above the thick green foliage of clustering trees. The car turned between high wide gateposts with crests carved on them. The branches of trees interlacing overhead made a tunnel of shade above a narrow winding lane.

From the tunnel they seemed to burst out into the brightness again and there was the castle, its solid walls softened here and there with the red-tinted leaves of Virginia creeper and the yellowish green of ivy. Below the green knoll on which the castle had been built borders of flowers, red, white and purple asters, orange marigolds,

Golden Rod, pink and white phlox blazed in a brilliant clash of colours.

The driveway wound round to the back of the castle where the original Norman keep was preserved complete with water-filled moat. In a clearing opposite the draw-bridge two touring buses were parked and people from them were walking slowly across the bridge. Driving cautiously, Nuala inched the car over the bridge and into the courtyard, bringing the car to a stop near one of the walls.

'I'll take you into the room where you'll sleep tonight,' she said in her imperious way as she took Kate's case from the car. 'Sean, perhaps you'd like to go and see Mother? You'll find her in the . . .' She broke off, biting her lip. Ignoring her, Sean was walking away. 'Now where's he off to?' she muttered. 'Oh, well, I've no time to go running after him now,' she added, smiling at Kate. 'Come on, this way.'

They went in through a thick wooden door and after a bewildering walk along a series of stone passages they arrived at a stairway that spiralled upwards inside a turret.

'Has your family always owned the castle?' Kate asked as she climbed the stairs after Nuala.

'No. My father bought it for a few thousand pounds twenty years ago, when it came on the market. It didn't have a roof then. He put in central heating, restored the roof and modernised the plumbing.' Nuala chuckled. 'He made his money selling scrap iron and other metals and it gives him quite a kick to think he owns a castle. In the summer he leases the oldest part of it to a tourist development company that puts on entertainment for foreign tourists. This year Guy Burke, who manages the entertainment department of the company, asked me to produce and perform in the pageant of song and poetry you'll hear after the banquet. I jumped at the chance because it meant I could be employed and keep an eye on Sean at the same time.'

'But how did you know Sean was going to be at Moyvalla for the summer?' Kate asked breathlessly as they reached the top of the stairs.

'I brought him there myself from the hospital,' Nuala replied, opening another sturdy oak door. 'Someone had to help him and look after him when he was discharged from hospital,' she added, with a critical glance at Kate, 'and I was the only person around who seemed to care about him.'

The room they went into was circular and had a narrow latticed window. On the bare stone walls hung colourful tapestries depicting knights on horseback and ladies in long gowns and high pointed hats. There was a huge fourposter bed covered with green and gold damask. A thick hand-knotted Wilton Royal carpet covered most of the floor.

'I hope you'll be comfortable here,' said Nuala, putting Kate's case down on the bench at the end of the bed. 'The bed isn't as antique as it looks, the mattress is modern and well sprung. You'll find a small washroom through that door over there. Dad spared no expense in the arrange-ments for the guest rooms because he likes to entertain V.I.P.s here.' She turned away to the door and then looked back. 'You've told Sean you're going to arrange for a divorce, haven't you?' she said.

'Yes. Did he tell you?'

'No. But I can guess by the way he's behaving. Telling him has made all the difference, roused him out of that awful lethargy. He was much more like himself when we were talking just before you came out of Moyvalla House.' Nuala's smile was warm and brilliant. 'Thanks, Kate,' she added softly. 'For both of us. I'm glad you came to see him. Now I'm sure he and I will be able to get back on our old footing. Make yourself comfortable now. Sorry to rush off but we begin promptly at six and I have to change into my costume.'

'But how will I find my way to the banquet?' exclaimed Kate, laughing. 'I've no idea where it's being held and wouldn't know how to find any other place in the castle after coming here.'

'I'll send one of the folk singers to fetch you,' replied Nuala, and left the room.

Half an hour later Kate opened the door to find a young man dressed in a green hooded jerkin which he wore with long dark green hose outside. He introduced himself as Liam Rosse, leader of the folksinging group known as the Green Folk, and said he had been sent by Nuala to take Kate to the banquet.

'Nuala says you've been to the festival at Ennis,' he added. 'How did it go?'

Pleased to find herself in the company of a kindred spirit, Kate told him about the festival as they left the turret and crossed the courtyard to the old Norman keep where the banquet and pageant were taking place. As he left her to follow the line of tourists who were entering the doorway Liam whispered,

'See you after the pageant is over. You can come back to the barn where the group is living while they're performing here and sing us some of the songs you know and we'll sing you the ones we know, make a night of it.'

'I'd like to,' she said.

Just inside the doorway, wearing an emerald green velvet gown with a low square neckline that revealed the smooth white skin of her throat and breast, Nuala stood greeting the dinner guests. Kate was guided to her place by one of the waitresses, a young woman dressed in a brightly coloured short full skirt, banded at the hem with black, a square-necked white blouse and a black shawl, the ends of which were tucked into the waistband of the skirt.

Seated on a long bench behind a long refectory table, Kate looked round the hall. All the tables were arranged around the walls and the diners sat on one side of them only so that the space in the middle of the hall was left clear for a small wooden circular stage with steps on either side of it and everyone could see the performance. From the high-beamed ceiling silken banners embroidered with different devices hung. Thick white candles in pewter candlesticks flickered on the tables and fire leapt in the wide stone fireplace.

Like the surroundings, the menu was truly medieval. There was *Sew Lumbarda*, a thick fish soup, while the main course was *Chekyns in Browet*—capons simmered in red wine. Mead was served in big pewter goblets.

'Mead is made from fermented honey and was drunk long ago by the Celtic people,' Nuala announced from her place at the head table. 'And there's a story connected with it, that I like to think is true, about a fifteenth-century custom of this country. It is told that in those days newly married couples drank only mead for one month or moon after their wedding and from that custom is derived the word honeymoon.' Picking up her goblet, she raised it high. 'I'd like to give you a toast. To all those couples here who are on their honeymoon, whether it's their first, second or even third one!'

The toast and the laughter that went with it broke down the barriers of shyness which had kept most of the diners fairly quiet during the first part of the banquet, and Kate discovered that she was sitting between two sisters, two elderly women from the United States who were excited by this, their first visit to the country from which their great-grandparents had emigrated in the nineteenth century.

A butler dressed in doublet and hose called for more mead. The goblets were replenished and the sound of talking voices grew louder. Candlelight flickered on faces. Firelight danced on the ancient stone walls. Across the room Kate caught site of Sean, head inclined attentively as he listened to a pretty blonde girl with a golden tan who was seated next to him, and for a few moments she was transported back in time and place to the restaurant in San Cristobal with firelight dancing on stone walls, and candlelight flickering on Sean's face as he had glanced sideways at the golden beauty of the American woman who had sat at the next table, and she felt once again the bewildering sharp pang of jealousy she had felt then, wishing suddenly he was sitting by her, looking and listening to her. Impatient with the feeling, she turned to one of the women sitting beside her, showing an interest, and was soon hearing all about the American's home in Washington, D.C.

At last the empty plates were removed from the tables. More mead was poured into goblets and a few candles were extinguished. From somewhere among the ceiling beams a spotlight shone down on the small stage. A hush came over the diners. The entertainment was about to begin.

The young men and women who had so recently waited on table now became performers and in speech and song they told the story of the castle, which was in effect the story of Ireland from the very earliest times. On the tiny stage scenes from the life of the people who had lived in the castle were acted out, some tragic, some comic and some downright romantic. At one time Nuala was the Irish maid, the only survivor of her family after the Celtic fort had been destroyed by Norman invaders and, held spellbound by her beauty and the richness of her voice, they listened to her pleading with the Norman knight who had defeated her people, sighing sentimentally when he was in his turn defeated by her, staying to marry her, to build the actual castle keep in which the play was being acted and to found the family that had owned the castle until recent times.

Enthralled by the singing and the acting, Kate never looked away from the small stage until the entertainment came to an end. Then after saying goodbye to the American ladies who were leaving with the other tourists to board the bus which would take them back to their hotels, she went over to the group of folk singers. Out of the corners of her eyes she noted that Sean was also leaving the hall with Nuala and some other people. Nuala's arm was crooked possessively through one of his.

In the stone barn which had been converted into living quarters for the summer entertainers she joined happily in the folk singing. Although there was a varied selection of instruments, guitars, penny whistles, a fiddle or two and even an electric dulcimer, most of the singers preferred to sing unaccompanied in true folk song style. Many of the songs were traditional Irish, Scots, Welsh or English, with some from the States and Canada. But some were original, the lyrics made up by the singer about some recent event or experience and often sung to an old tune.

The moon was high and full, sailing in a sky of midnight blue, when Kate at last returned to the castle, where squares of yellow light patterned the dark bulk of the walls, indicating that some people were still up and about. As she climbed the winding stairway of the turret she hummed one of the tunes which had pleased her. As usual, in the company of people like herself who loved to sing, folk songs had brought her some measure of tranquillity and she had forgotten her problems for a while.

But the sound of distant laughter welling up from a room in the castle reminded her that Sean was somewhere in the building with Nuala, and at once all peace of mind fled, ripped away by sharp sword-like jealousy. Digging her teeth into her lower lip to prevent herself from crying out with the pain, she plodded doggedly up the stairs.

By staying away from her all through the banquet, by going off with Nuala afterwards without a look in her direction or a word to her, Sean had made it very obvious that he was going to renew his affair with the woman now that he knew that his marriage to herself would be dissolved.

Well, she didn't care, Kate thought defiantly. They were welcome to each other. In many ways they were very alike. Both had bold hawk-like features, both were pale eyed, dark-haired Celts. Both were strong-willed, ambitious, thoroughly selfish and egotistical, riding roughshod over people like herself, not caring whom they hurt as long as they got their own way.

And she wasn't going to lose any sleep thinking about them. She would sleep well tonight and tomorrow she would go on her way, back to England, refreshed by all that she had heard and seen in this lovely green land.

The hinges of the heavy door of the bedroom creaked as she pushed it open. Moonlight shining through the latticed window made a pattern of silvery diamonds on the carpet and it gleamed softly on the shirt of the man who was lying on the bed.

CHAPTER SEVEN

TENSION quivering along her nerves, Kate closed the door quietly and leaned back against it still staring at the bed. No she hadn't made a mistake. The moonlight wasn't deceiving her. Sean was lying on top of the bedcover, and he seemed to be very fast asleep because the sound of the door opening and closing hadn't disturbed him.

Pushing away from the door, she walked slowly over to the bed and looked down at him. Silvered by moonlight, his profile was distinct against the darkness of the bedcover. Her glance lingering on the way his hair curved against his temple, on the darkness of the lashes against his cheek, on the relaxed line of his mouth now he was asleep, on the strong jut of his jaw, she sank down on the edge of the bed. She had liked the way he looked from the first moment of seeing him that hot day by the fountain at the Santa Rosa Mission, and she supposed that on the physical level the attraction had been strong, beyond her control.

It was still strong. Why not admit it? Why not admit that she was having difficulty now in keeping her hands to herself? She wanted to reach and touch him, stroke the hair back from his brow, lay her cheek against his, wake him with a kiss. The urge to do so was pulsing through her, filling her with its heat. It was a desire she had never experienced for any other man and she couldn't imagine herself feeling this way with any other man. It was a part of love.

'Sean,' she whispered, and touched his shoulder tentatively, withdrawing her hand from its cotton-sheathed warmth quickly as if she had been burned. 'Wake up, please!'

His chest rose and fell as he took a deep sighing breath, he frowned slightly, then his eyes opened and he looked right at her his eyes gleaming between slitted lids.

'Kate?' he murmured.

'Yes, of course.'

'You keep late hours. Where have you been?' He pushed up on one elbow, coming so close to her that she shifted back along the bed, her heart thudding.

'With the folk singers, at the barn where they stay. We sang songs to each other. I thought you'd gone back to Moyvalla. Or . . . or that you were with Nuala. I saw you leave the banqueting hall with her.'

Sean lay back against the pillows, hands beneath his head supporting it. In the moonlight Kate could see quite clearly the sardonic twist to his mouth.

'She insisted on me going to see her mother. There was quite a party going on in the private part of the castle, some of Nuala's theatre friends and a well-known film producer who wants to make a film of the castle with Nuala starring in it,' he said. The twist to his mouth became more marked. 'I couldn't stand their way of talking, so I left. I was going back to Moyvalla, then I remembered I hadn't said goodbye to you, so I came up here.'

'How did you know Nuala had given me this room?' asked Kate.

'I didn't. I found my way by instinct,' he drawled. 'You weren't here. I felt tired, so I decided to lie down and wait for you.' He paused, then moved suddenly, sitting up and shifting closer to her again. 'I'm glad you've come at last,' he whispered.

Smelling slightly of the honeyed sweetness of mead, his breath wafted tantalisingly across her mouth. His shirt was unbuttoned to the waist and she could feel the warmth of his body beating out to her.

'You've been drinking again,' she accused softly, gripping her hands tightly together in case they betrayed her and reached out to slide under the edges of his shirt and curve about his body.

'Only the mead at the banquet. Although I have to admit it's heady stuff I've slept off the effects of it,' he murmured 'I liked that story Nuala told about it, didn't you? About the origin of the word honeymoon.' His fingers found and stroked delicately along the angle of her jaw. 'Remember our honeymoon, Kate?' he added

'We . . . we . . . didn't have one,' she said breathlessly, her heart seeming to fill her throat with its flutter. The effort to control the desire to touch him was making her ache inside. 'We were together only one night.'

'But it was a honey of a night, wasn't it?' His hand slid down from her cheek to the bow that fastened the neck of her dress. With a quick flick it was undone and his fingers slid inside the neck of the dress, warm against the hollow at the base of her throat as he slipped undone the top button. 'We could make tonight wonderful, too. Together,' he added suggestively.

She touched him at last, her fingers curling round his hand trying to pull it away from the bodice of her dress even though she was leaning towards him.

'Sean, please behave! It's late and . . .'

'Sure, I'll behave,' he said with a laugh as the last button on the bodice was slipped undone. 'I'll behave like a husband does on his honeymoon.'

His lips touched hers gently, coaxingly, then withdrew before she could respond as he slid the dress from one of her shoulders. Then they burned briefly in the curve between her neck and her shoulder, melting the last of her resistance. Yet still she held back from commitment.

'Sean, we shouldn't,' she whispered, even while her hands crept up his chest, the tips of her fingers and the cushioned pads of her palms finding pleasure in the tangle of hairs on his chest and then in the smoothness of the skin covering his shoulders.

'Why shouldn't we, if we want to?' His lips teased hers gently. 'And you're not going to tell me you don't want to now. I'll know you're lying if you do.'

'But . . . it won't mean anything . . . if we're going to be divorced.' She had intended to withdraw as she made the complaint, slip from his arms and slide off the bed, retreat to safety, but from the depths of her came a response to the tender torment of his roving fingertips which was much stronger than her will, a sudden turbulence whirling her along towards complete surrender.

'It will always mean something to me,' Sean murmured. His voice was steady, but she could hear he was having difficulty in controlling his breath. 'And remember it has nothing to do with us being married, Kate, nothing at all,' he mocked, tilting her chin up. 'You didn't really believe I would let you leave tomorrow without giving you something to remember, did you?'

Their lips met gently at first. The kiss was slow and relaxed like the rhythm of the sea on the sand, retreating, then approaching again, deepening and lengthening as both of them tried to find and reach the essence of the other. Gradually they lay down together on the bed, hands sweeping away clothing, fingers arousing passion one by one, shaping within each other a growing, aching hunger.

'It'll be better this time,' Sean murmured. 'This time we go side by side, neither of us leading. You're all woman now, strong and beautiful, rounded and soft, not a skinny naïve girl needing to be taught. And how shall I describe your beauty, your skin as soft as down, your hair like raw silk, your lips tender as rose-petals, your breasts as . . . Oh, Kate,' he gasped thickly, and his lips parted hers in a kiss that both demanded and worshipped, and after that nothing mattered any more as all the restless cravings of the past two years gathered together and united in a wondrous, crashing fanfare. Brass blared, drums rolled and the moon-dappled darkness seemed to shake and burst apart.

Kate woke up slowly, swimming to the surface of sleep, becoming aware of the world little by little. First the feel of the warm hard male body lying on her left arm, then of the strange tang of hair in her nostrils, the faint smell of his skin, the sound of his breathing.

Daylight beat against her eyelids and she opened them to glance downwards. Black as jet, glinting with silver threads, Sean's hair was spread over her shoulder and he was a heavy supine weight on her left arm. He was still sunk in the deep all-healing sleep induced by the satiation of passion.

Was that all it had been? The satisfaction of physical desire? Nothing else? Had there been no meeting of spirits, no real union? Kate groaned inwardly in sudden dreariness as she managed to slide her arm from beneath him. She should have turned and fled from the room as soon as she had seen him lying on the bed. She shouldn't have let desire overwhelm her. Even now she was reluctant to leave the bed. She felt warm as if she were glowing inside and she wanted to snuggle down beside Sean, caress him into wakefulness. . . . Oh God—she flung herself from the bed and began to pick up scattered clothing from the floor. It was late and she must be on her way to Dublin. She must get back to Westcourt in time for that interview.

She had washed and was almost dressed when there was

a sharp knock on the door. Going over to it, she called through the panels,

'Who is it?'

'Nuala. I've brought you some tea and toast.'

Help! Kate's glance flicked to the bed. Sean was still asleep.

'Just a minute,' she called, and running back to the bed flung the bedcover over Sean, covering him completely, then went back and opened the door. Still in a dressing gown, her black hair hanging over one shoulder in a thick braid, Nuala stood there holding a tray on which there was a small silver teapot, milk jug and sugar basin, a china cup and saucer and a plate of toast. She walked into the room and set the tray down on the writing table under the window.

'I'll be leaving for Dunane in about twenty minutes,' she said briskly, while with one hand to her mouth Kate stared in consternation at Sean's shirt lying in a crumpled heap on the floor and his trousers casually draped over the bed end. What would she say if Nuala noticed them?

But Nuala was going straight back to the door.

'Did you sleep well?' she asked, turning back to look at Kate.

'Yes, thank you. I enjoyed the pageant and the folk singing afterwards.'

'Brendan, Liam, Colleen and the rest enjoyed you too. They say you have a lovely voice.' Nuala's intensely blue gaze swept over Kate, from the coronet of red hair to the long line of thigh and leg. 'You're good-looking too. Have you ever thought of making a career out of entertainment?'

'No.' Kate shook her head. 'I enjoy the career I have, thank you.'

'So you're not dependent on Sean.'

'Certainly not!' Kate's head went up and her shoulders

straightened. 'And never have been.'

'Did you see him last night, after you left the barn to come here?'

'Why do you ask?' Kate hoped she wouldn't change colour and that she would be able to continue to look Nuala in the eyes.

'I asked him to stay the night here, but he must have decided to go back to Moyvalla, because he isn't in the room I offered to him and the bed hasn't been slept in. I hope that's what happened to him, anyway,' added Nuala. 'He was in a very strange mood and I was worried about him. That's why I suggested he should stay. But I mustn't keep you talking. You'll want to be on your way.'

Nuala went out and the door closed. Letting out a sigh of relief, Kate poured tea and chewed toast, staring out of the window at the curve of the river she could see gleaming in the sunlight. Behind her there was the rustle of bedclothes. She looked round quickly. Sean had thrown back the bed-cover and had turned on to his other side.

She drank some more tea, finished dressing, repacked her suitcase and locked it. She made up her face and slung on her raincoat. Once again she was ready to go and this time no one was going to stop her from leaving. With luck her car should be ready and she should be in Dublin by late afternoon.

Slowly she wandered over to the bed and gazed down at Sean. Her case dropped with a thud at her feet. The side of the mattress sagged as she sat down on it and leaned over him. She didn't want to leave him. She ached to stay with him. Why? So they could make love again? Or because she loved him? What was love? Did she know? She had thought she had known in San Marco, but she could see now that what she had felt for him had been merely hero-worship of the knight errant who had come to rescue her. The feeling had faded and she had believed it had died when she had discovered he had faults like anyone else; when she had learned the hard way that she didn't come first with him.

Sean opened one eye and looked right at her. She stood up and picking up her case walked to the door.

'Nuala is waiting to take me to Dunane, so I'll say goodbye,' she said coolly.

'Wait a minute!' he said sharply.

Kate looked back. He was sitting up, shoulders and chest bare above the sheet.

'I haven't time. I must go or I'll never get to Westcourt tonight,' she said, and turned the doorknob. 'Goodbye.'

'Goodbye, Kate.' He spoke very quietly and she turned to look at him. He was lying back against the pillow, arms behind his head, taking his ease. 'And good luck with the interview. Take care on the road.'

'I will.' She stepped through the doorway and closed the door behind her.

Feeling as if she was being torn in two one part of her remaining there in the turret room with Sean, the other part on its way already, winging over the Irish Sea to England, she hurried down the winding stairway, her case bumping against her legs.

In the sunlit courtyard Nuala was just starting her car. Out over the drawbridge they went and down the tree-arched driveway. The blue water of the estuary wimpled in the wind and the land on the other side stretched away, a hundred shades of green, as far as the hazy blue line of hills.

Nuala was in a bad mood. It showed in her driving as she snatched at gears. A fierce scowl darkened her face, pulling her eyebrows together to make a straight black bar above the bridge of her nose.

'I phoned Moyvalla,' she said abruptly. 'There was no answer.'

'He could still be sleeping,' said Kate, trying to sound indifferent, thinking of Sean as she had last seen him, at ease in the bed in the turret room, not at all disturbed because she was leaving him. 'Or he could have gone fishing,' she added.

'Mmm, I suppose so,' muttered Nuala. 'I hope you're right. I think I'll drive over to the house when I've dropped you at McCormic's just to make sure.' She glanced at Kate. 'You meant what you said yesterday, didn't you? You are going to arrange for a divorce when you get back to England?'

'I meant what I said.'

'Has Sean agreed?' Nuala persisted, as they surged across the hump-backed bridge towards the village.

'He hasn't disagreed,' Kate replied. Over the parapet of the bridge she could see the water swirling in dark circles over hidden rocks as the tide flooded. From the small harbour a fishing boat glided out, then was hidden from view as the car turned into a narrow street that twisted uphill past crouching cottages.

'Will you marry again?' Nuala asked.

'I'm not sure.' Kate was relieved to notice they had arrived at a long grey shed outside which there was a petrol pump and the small red car.

'Here we are. I hope your car goes,' said Nuala. 'Would you like me to wait while you find out?'

'Would you mind?'

'Not at all. Then if it won't go I can drive you into Ennis where you can get a bus or a train to take you on your way.' She smiled suddenly and brilliantly. 'Notice how keen I am to get rid of you! As far as I'm concerned you spell danger to my friendship with Sean.'

'Don't you trust him?' asked Kate.

'Not with someone as attractive as you are who happens

to be married to him into the bargain.'

Martin McCormic was a wisp of a man, dressed in oil-marked dungarees. He had a weathered face and eyes like bits of blue sky and he spoke with a thick brogue which Kate had difficulty in understanding so that she was glad Nuala was there.

'He says there was very little wrong with your car and you could have had it yesterday afternoon,' said Nuala, who was frowning fiercely again.

'But Sean said the electrics needed drying out.'

'Sure they were fine, just fine,' said Martin. 'It was the battery that was down. You get in now and see if she starts.'

The car started straight away, and after paying Martin and saying goodbye to Nuala Kate drove away, glad to be mobile again, but more than a little irritated with Sean for deceiving her over the matter of the car. She could have left yesterday and if she had last night wouldn't have happened. Physical desire wouldn't have got the better of both of them, entangling them in its sensual snare.

It was all Uncle Hugh's fault. If he hadn't invited her to Moyvalla she wouldn't have seen Sean again and she wouldn't have fallen in love with him again. When she reached Dublin, if she had time, she would go to see Hugh and give him a piece of her mind!

She drove as fast as she dared along the coast road and didn't slow down at all as she approached Moyvalla. In the rear view mirror she noticed the black Volkswagen turn into the driveway and wondered what sort of blarney Sean would use to talk himself out of trouble when Nuala found out he had stayed the night at the castle after all. Laughter welled up in her as she recalled how she had thrown the bedcover over him. She had behaved no better than a housemaid caught with a man in her bed by the mistress of the castle!

There was little traffic on the road at that time of day and within an hour she had reached Ennis and was turning towards Limerick and by noon was dipping down towards the shining blue ribbon of the River Shannon. The walls of the castle known as King John's bulked darkly over the sunlit water, tempting her to stop and explore, but there was no time to spare. Leaving the Viking city which over the years had withstood so many sieges from so many different enemies, she drove out along the road which twists its way across the emerald-coloured land to Dublin.

It was late afternoon when she eventually drove into the city, dodging between double-decker buses. People swarmed along the pavements, exhaust fumes clouded the air and the traffic seemed to be irreparably tangled. Kate's neck and shoulders ached from the long drive, and, hungry because she hadn't stopped to eat in her headlong flight from Dunane, she turned down a convenient side street and pulled into the curb in front of a public house. She had just taken out the map book supplied by the car rental agency to consult it, when a motorbike drew up alongside. On it was a uniformed Garda, an Irish policeman. Kate let down the window.

'You can't park here, miss,' he said.

'I've only stopped to look at a map,' she explained.

'Where are you going?'

'I'm looking for Milford Drive.'

He pushed back his uniform cap and scratched at his head.

'I'm thinking that's a good way from here,' he said. 'If you like to be following me I'll be showing you the way meself.'

'Oh, are you sure it won't be too much trouble?' exclaimed Kate.

'No trouble at all. At least it'll be less trouble than trying to give you directions,' he replied with a grin. 'Are you ready now?'

Through street after street of the glutted downtown area of the city he led her and out to a pleasant residential area of old houses with lace-curtained windows which were situated at the end of long narrow gardens. Right to the house where Hugh lived he led her, not leaving until he was sure she had parked correctly. Kate thanked him, charmed by his native friendliness and willingness to go out of his way, and opening the small wrought-iron gate set in the low brick wall in front of the house walked up the narrow path between borders of purple and white asters, brilliant pink phlox and glowing orange marigolds.

Geraldine O'Connor, an old white linen hat on her head, was on her hands and knees in the garden trimming the edge of the lawn she had been cutting.

'Hello, Aunt Gerry. Is Uncle Hugh at home?' Kate asked.

Geraldine stiffened and turned her head cautiously to glance up.

'Saints preserves us!' she exclaimed. 'And where have you come from?'

'Today I've come from Dunane. It's not far from Moyvalla House, and I'm sure you've heard of that,' said Kate wearily, rubbing the back of her neck to try and get the stiffness out of it. She had an ache too in the small of her back and her legs felt as if they were stuffed with sawdust, they were so numb. 'I'm sorry if I gave you a fright, Aunt Gerry.'

'You've driven all that way today?' exclaimed Geraldine, getting to her feet. Small and plump, she had round brown eyes which gave her double-chinned face a perpetually innocent expression. 'Why?'

'I have to be in Westcourt by tomorrow. I'm catching a

plane over this evening. Is Hugh at home?'

'Of course he is, pounding away at the typewriter, even though it is one of the best summer days we've had. Come away now into the house and I'll be putting the kettle on.' The brown eyes became suddenly shrewd as they eyed Kate's face. 'You're looking as if you're in need of more than tea. Are you sure now you can't stay the night and catch a plane in the morning?'

'Quite sure.'

They went up a flight of narrow steps to the double front doors of the Edwardian house. As they entered the high hallway Geraldine stood for a moment at the foot of the stairs to shout,

'Hugh, come downstairs! There's someone to see you. You'll never guess who it is.' She turned and winked at Kate. 'That should bring him,' she added. 'Come into the kitchen now.'

The kitchen was big and full of sunshine from the west. Like the one in the house the O'Connors had owned at Hampstead it was the hub of the house, the place where everyone gathered and where everything happened. Indoor plants hung about it in corners and in front of windows. In a cage a big black and yellow parrot squawked a lewd greeting to Kate. From a big cretonne-covered chesterfield Geraldine swept two cats who had been sleeping there and told Kate to sit down, then began to busy herself taking crockery from the cupboard.

'Moyvalla House,' she mused. 'Now why should that sound familiar?'

'Hugh spent a few days there at the beginning of August,' said Kate with a sigh, leaning back and closing her eyes.

'So he did. Went for the fishing, he said.' Geraldine clattered spoons. 'But that wouldn't be why you were there. You don't fish, do you, Kate?'

'No, I don't. I went there because Hugh invited me to go there,' snapped Kate crossly. Sometimes Géraldine's absentmindedness could be very irritating.

'Now why would he be doing that?' asked Geraldine.

'That's what I want to know,' said Kate acidly, and just then the kitchen door was pushed open and Hugh came in.

'Kate! What the hell are you doing here? Why aren't you at Moyvalla with Sean?' he demanded. Dressed in disreputable grey flannels and a V-necked jersey which had seen better days, his greying reddish hair in wild disorder with running his fingers through it, he came across, sat down beside her and planted a kiss of welcome on her cheek. 'Didn't you get my letter inviting you there?'

'Yes, I did get your letter, and I wrote back telling you I would be there the day before yesterday and would stay only one night,' she retorted. 'Did you get my letter?'

'Sean sent it on here,' he said, studying her closely. 'I couldn't stay there until you arrived.'

'Don't you mean you had no intention of staying until I arrived?' she flared. 'You tricked me into going there! Why didn't you tell me Sean would be there?'

'Well, you said you wanted to see him, so I thought . . .'

'I didn't,' she interrupted him hotly. 'I asked you only if you could find out where he was so I could get in touch with him. I didn't want to see him. I didn't, I didn't!' To her own surprise she burst suddenly into tears and flung herself against him. 'Oh, Uncle Hugh,' she sobbed, 'I didn't want to see him again. I only wanted to know where he was.'

'Now, now, there, there,' he murmured comfortingly as he held her in his arms.

'The kettle has boiled,' said Geraldine in a similar comforting way, 'and the tea will soon be ready. I'm thinking you've overdone it, Kate, driving all that way on your own. And I wouldn't be at all surprised if you didn't stop to eat on the way. Come to the table now. There's fresh scones and strawberry jam I've made myself this year from the berries we grew in the garden. Hugh, she says she has to catch a plane to London this evening, but I think it would be best if she stayed the night, don't you?'

'No, I can't,' said Kate stubbornly, drying her cheeks on her hand and going to the table. 'I have an interview tomorrow morning. But I told you about that in my letter.'

'So you did, so you did,' agreed Hugh, going over to the mantelpiece to select a pipe from the rack there.

The tea was strong and reviving, the scones of the melt-in-the-mouth variety and the strawberry jam solid with teeth-cheating fruit. While Kate drank and ate Geraldine kept up a flow of talk about her two children, saying how she and Hugh expected to be grandparents in a month's time, a topic which led her to ask with seeming naturalness about Kate's marital status.

'And now that you've seen Sean again, what are your plans? Are you going to live together?'

'No. I . . . I'm going to divorce him,' Kate answered in a rush. 'That was why I wanted to know where he was so that the lawyer could contact him. It could have been done without me seeing him again.'

There was a heavy silence in which they both stared at her and she knew she had come up against their intense disapproval.

'Sean never wanted to be married. He married me only to help me get out of San Marco,' she muttered defensively. 'He wanted me to have the marriage dissolved as soon as I got back to England. I'll only be doing what he wants, after all.' She looked at Hugh, meeting his eyes defiantly. 'Why did you do it, Uncle Hugh?' she asked again. 'Why did you invite me to his house without telling me he would be there?'

'Yes, why did you, Hugh?' Geraldine added.

'I did it for the best,' he replied, puffing hard on his pipe to get it going. 'I didn't like what I found over there on the west coast one little bit. Didn't like it at all.' He puffed out a cloud of smoke and shook his head from side to side. 'Since you'd made no attempt to get in touch with him after he'd been hurt in the accident he'd more or less assumed that you'd put an end to the marriage. But he wasn't happy and he wasn't recovering as rapidly as he should because he was drinking too much. So I decided it was time you and he met again, to sort things out between you.' Through the cloud of grey tobacco smoke he gave Kate a straight sharp glance. 'Why didn't you get in touch with him after the accident?'

'Because I didn't know there'd been an accident. I didn't know he was in hospital. All I knew was that he hadn't come to see me at Christmas as he'd said he would.' Kate took a deep shaky breath. 'I wish I'd done what he suggested in the first place now. I wish I'd had the marriage dissolved as soon as I returned to England from Mexico, and then . . . then . . . none of this would have happened. We . . . we would both be free.' Her voice wobbled and she had to blink back tears. Quickly she pushed to her feet. 'I'll have to go if I'm going to catch the plane.'

'From the sound of things it seems your attempt at playing at being God hasn't turned out too well, Hugh O'Connor,' Geraldine observed dryly.

'You're making a mistake, Kate, if you go through with a divorce now,' said Hugh urgently. 'You haven't given your marriage a chance to work.'

'Yes, I have. I've given it two years and not once in that time has Sean written or attempted to see me. Only last

Christmas, and I know now that he was only coming to see me to find out if I'd done anything about a divorce, for nothing else. He wasn't coming then because he loved me. He didn't marry me because he loved me and I see now that I've expected too much from him, far more than he's been able to give.' She took another deep breath. 'I'll never make that mistake again, you can be sure of that.'

She could see that they were upset by what she was saying. Both staunch in their religious faith, they believed in marriage and family as the cornerstones of the society in which they lived and found it hard to condone divorce. Yet when Kate left the house they both embraced her warmly and asked her to come back again.

She caught the plane with only a few minutes to spare and spent the hour's flight thinking over what Hugh had said about Sean. It was strange that both Hugh and Nuala had been worried by Sean's uncharacteristic behaviour but had different explanations for it. Nuala had said his unhappiness was due to the fact that he was still married and didn't want to be married. Hugh had suggested that Sean's poor state of mind was caused by his uncertainty concerning his relation to herself.

The sooner he was free of her the better for him. The better for her too. The marriage which had taken place in San Marco in such desperate circumstances was only an encumbrance to both of them, making it difficult for them to become real friends. As soon as the interview was over she would go and see Paul Holgate, give him Sean's address at Moyvalla so that he could write to Sean.

It was eleven o'clock when she reached Westcourt and the moon was high in the sky, silvering the clouds which were floating above it. Glad to have reached her destination, Kate climbed the stairs to her flat and let herself in. Going straight to the bedroom, she dropped her suitcase and began to undress. After a quick wash in the bathroom she returned to crawl into bed, sure she would sleep at once.

Hours later she was still awake, watching the moonlight fingering the edges of the drawn curtains, thinking of Sean. Meeting him again, being with him for two whole nights and a day, feeling his hand on hers, her pulse leaping to the look in his eyes, had been too much to bear and she had run away, back to the safety of her job at Netherfield, the possibility of promotion and her way of life in Westcourt where he had never been.

When he had walked away from her at Mexico City airport and had not entered her life for two whole years, he had freed her from the promises she had made to him. In leaving him at Dunane Castle that morning, she had freed him and had thought to free herself again. But it was a ghastly freedom, arid and bitter. Lying here remembering and coveting his mouth, longing for the warm thrust of his body against hers, aching for the cool fingertip delight of his hands, was to die a little.

Was it too much to hope he was feeling the same? Could he possibly love her as, she realised now, she still loved him? Surely being in love should mean looking at everything through each other's eyes and knowing it. It should mean tasting and feeling everything together. It should not mean this terrible gnawing hunger for a rare and tantalising fruit.

She slept at last and woke early. Shaking off the dreaded lethargy of desolation, she prepared for the interview and arrived at Netherfield in good time. To her surprise the interview was very brief. Miss Forbes and the members of the board of trustees of the school who made up the interviewing committee were all very pleasant and complimented her on the work she had done the previous year. But they asked no questions about how she would organise the music department or what plans she had for the Christmas concert and the springtime stage musical. After thanking her for attending the interview and telling her she would be informed by post during the next week as to the success of her application Miss Forbes dismissed her.

Next day Kate travelled up to London to see Paul Holgate. She gave him Sean's address at Moyvalla and instructed him to write to Sean suggesting a divorce by consent. She did some shopping and returned to Westcourt. Barry was there, waiting for her outside.

'How was the trip to Ireland?' he asked, taking her parcels from her and then following her up the stairs to her flat.

'Fine. I enjoyed the festival.'

'Did you see your uncle?' In the living-room he set down her parcels on the sofa.

'Yes.' Kate took off the broad-brimmed hat she had been wearing and unpinned her hair, letting it fall about her shoulders.

'Did he have the information you wanted?' Barry persisted, following her into the kitchenette where she proceeded to fill the kettle with water.

'What information?' she asked cautiously.

'Kierly's whereabouts.'

'Oh, yes, Paul is writing to Sean today.'

'Good. How did the interview go at Netherfield?'

'It was puzzling.' She struck a match and held it to the gas burner. 'Everyone was so pleasant—too pleasant. I got the feeling they weren't really interested in me.'

'Any plans for the rest of your holidays?'

'Not really.'

'Then why don't you join Carol and me, my sister and her husband on a short cruise across the Channel to France? We'd be back by the middle of next week. The weather forecast is good.'

Kate looked around, remembering the agony of the previous night. Anything would be better than having to put up with her own company and wishful thinking for the next week. Sailing would take her mind off her troubles.

'I'd love to come,' she said. 'What time should I be ready?'

From every point of view the week's cruise was perfect. The weather was warm and sunny with enough wind to keep the boat moving, the company, Carol, Barry, Dora and Jack Harper, cheerful and undemanding. Yet Kate was as eager to return to Westcourt as she had been to leave it and when she arrived at her flat on her return she lost no time in collecting the post which had arrived for her.

First she looked for a letter from Sean, but none of the envelopes was addressed in his bold sloping handwriting. Next she found and opened the envelope bearing the crest of Netherfield Private School for Girls. The letter was brief and polite. It thanked her for showing an interest in the position of head of the music department and informed her that she had not been appointed. A Miss Celia Fromsett, a Doctor of Music, had been awarded the position and it was hoped that she would meet Miss Fromsett at a staff meeting to be held at the school three days before the beginning of term.

CHAPTER EIGHT

OUTSIDE the long windows of the music room at Netherfield the last few leaves whirled slowly down from the trees. It was almost the end of November, yet the weather was still surprisingly mild. It had been a good autumn, weatherwise, thought Kate dully as she sat beside the grand piano only half listening to Carol Wyman stumbling through a study. It had in fact been an Indian summer with days of mellow sunshine drifting one into the other, and only recently had wind and rain come to snatch the bronze and yellow leaves from the trees and scatter them into wet brown heaps about the school grounds.

Nearly three months had gone by since she had left Sean at Dunane Castle. Three months and no word from him. Her head bent, Kate studied the flecks of brown and green in the tweed of her skirt, her ear vaguely registering the mistakes Carol was making, her mind storing them up until the girl had finished playing. Then and only then would she draw her pupil's attention to them and suggest how they could be corrected.

Usually she didn't allow Sean into her thoughts during the day time. Usually she was able to stop short of him by keeping busy. But she was tired, and she knew the reason. Not enough sleep because whenever the close of each day came she was unable to keep him out, and she spent her nights with him, in dreams and in thought. And now because she was feeling weak he was taking over in the daytime.

'Miss Lawson!' The voice was high and cool, the sound

of icicles tinkling together, and it belonged to Celia From-sett.

Straightening up, Kate turned towards the door and gave a wary glance at the woman who was now head of the music department. Slim and fair-haired, neat and precise, Celia Fromsett was about thirty. She wore large-lensed glasses which seemed to cover the top part of her small-featured face and which had soon earned her the name of The Owl from the girls attending the school. From the moment of meeting her Kate had disliked her. At first she had attributed her dislike to the possibility that she re-sented Celia because the woman had been appointed to the position she would have liked, but as the term had pro-gressed she had realised that the dislike was based on an instinctive recoil from someone who was hard and almost vicious in the treatment of pupils who did not come up to Celia's high standards of behaviour and musical ability.

Maybe it was because she was feeling tired now that all her irritation came boiling up to the surface and burst through her restraint, thought Kate as she rose slowly to her feet.

'Miss Fromsett, I realise that as head of the department you probably feel you can make demands on my time when you like, but this happens to be a private lesson taking place out of school hours and you have no right to interrupt it,' she said, feeling her face heating as her temper took over.

Behind the owl-like lenses Celia's pale eyes glinted like pools of frozen water as their glance swept over Kate and then slanted at Carol's blonde head as the girl continued to play the study, her fingers tripping over wrong notes.

'All right, Carol,' Celia said icily. 'That's enough. It's quite obvious to me that you haven't practised that piece. In fact I wonder if you ever practise the piano. It seems to

me that your father is wasting his money on paying for you
to have lessons. Your musical ability is nil. You're dismissed now. Go to your room.'

'But I haven't finished my lesson,' Carol complained,
turning on the piano stool to glare at Miss Fromsett. 'I'm
only going if Miss Lawson tells me it's over.'

'I've said it's over and that should be enough,' replied
Celia tautly. 'Now do as you're told. Go to your room. As
soon as it's possible I'll have a word with your father about
you giving up music.'

'But I don't want to give it up,' wailed Carol. 'I like
playing the piano, and I like being in the school orchestra.'
She turned anxiously to Kate, who saw tears glistening in
the girl's eyes.

'Carol, do as Miss Fromsett says,' said Kate, keeping a
hold on her temper and speaking as calmly as she could.
She even managed to smile at the girl. 'I'll see you
later.'

Carol gathered up her music and after another hostile
glare at Miss Fromsett and a watery smile at Kate she left
the room. In a room filled suddenly with mellow sunset
glow Kate faced Celia across the shiny surface of the grand
piano.

'That was unnecessary. Carol is a very sensitive child,'
she snapped. 'And being able to play the piano and perform
on the flute in the school orchestra as well has helped her
enormously to cope with certain problems in her life. I
don't know if you know, but her mother deserted her when
she was about eight and . . .'

'Miss Lawson,' Celia interrupted her, 'it's about time
you realised that the music department of this school does
not exist to provide occupational therapy or any other sort
of therapy for neurotics. If Carol is in need of that sort of
treatment she should be in another kind of school. She has

no musical talent and it's a waste of time and money giving her lessons.'

'I don't agree. She plays quite well. . . .'

'Quite well!' Celia's thin pink lips sneered. 'Mediocre, that's it, and I don't have time for mediocrity. I'm determined that every girl in this school who takes music shall be an above average performer. The chaff must be sorted out from the wheat, leaving only the best. Next spring Netherfield School orchestra and Netherfield School choir under my direction will attend and win national competitions and festivals, and that can't be done if girls like Carol are included in them.' Celia paused and lifted one thin shoulder in a dismissing shrug as she turned away. 'Anyway, I know you only encourage her to please her father because you're his mistress.'

Shock was like being hit in the face with ice-cold water. Kate gasped for breath. Then anger blazed up within her again, consuming all the restraint she had been imposing on herself when dealing with this woman. Suddenly she didn't care what she said to Celia. Suddenly it didn't matter if she laid her job at Netherfield on the line by speaking her mind.

'That's not true! I'm not Barry Wyman's mistress!' she flared.

'Expect me to believe that when everyone knows you spend your spare time in his company and are a frequent guest at his house? You spend weekends there,' taunted Celia.

'I've been a guest at Rosedene once this term, at the invitation of Mrs Wyman, his mother. And I wasn't the only guest and Carol was there at the time.'

'It seems to me you're protesting your innocence too much,' sneered Celia.

'And it seems to me you go out of your way to pry into matters that don't concern you,' retorted Kate, her head up, her dark eyes glinting with fiery lights, her hair flaming against the glow of sunset. 'How you managed to get the position you have in this school I can't understand. You may be a highly accomplished musician, but when it comes to handling people, especially adolescent girls, you haven't a clue. You're mean and spiteful. . . .'

'Aha, now it's all coming out,' jeered Celia, who was still as cool as when she had entered the room. 'You wanted the position as head of the department, didn't you? And you thought you had it in the bag. It must have been a great disappointment to you when your lover didn't come through and influence the interviewing committee in your favour. Well, since you're speaking your mind I might as well speak mine. I don't like having you working under me. Your discipline is lax and unless there's an attempt on your part to improve your standards of teaching I'll have to complain to Miss Forbes and insist on your resignation so that someone else can be appointed.'

'It's just possible I'll be doing some complaining myself about you!' Kate seethed, and snatching up her handbag she marched out of the room, feeling that if she stayed she might be sorry for anything she might do.

She felt sick as she walked through the dusk-filled assembly hall on her way to the headmistress's office. She would go and see Miss Forbes immediately and if necessary hand in her resignation. It would hurt to do so. It would mean she had been defeated by Celia Fromsett. It would mean giving up Netherfield and the friends she had made there among the girls and the staff.

She knocked on the door of the school secretary's room, opened it and put her head round. Karen Williams was still seated at her desk typing industriously.

'Is the Head in her office?' Kate asked.

'No. She's gone up to London for the evening,' replied Karen. A thickset woman with an impassive face and calm eyes, she was the rock on which the organisation of Nether-field was built. Her eyes narrowed as she looked at Kate. 'Anything I can do to help?'

Kate walked into the room and closed the door behind her. Now that her anger was dying down she was begin-ning to feel drained of all energy.

'I've just had the most awful set-to with Fromsett,' she admitted rather breathlessly. 'It's made me feel quite ill. Do you mind if I sit down?'

'Go ahead.' Karen frowned. 'Mmm, you do look a little white. Miss Drummond was saying the other day how tired you've been looking lately.'

'I didn't think the Drum noticed anything,' said Kate with a wan smile. Margery Drummond was the vice-headmistress and head of the English Department. A distinguished poetess, she appeared to be very absent-minded.

'Been to see a doctor?' asked Karen.

'No, I haven't,' said Kate, sitting down.

'You should, you know. You might be anaemic and need some blood shots.'

'I haven't been sleeping too well lately, that's all,' said Kate defensively.

'Something on your mind?' queried Karen shrewdly. 'Not too happy, are you, working with Celia Fromsett?'

'Does it show?'

'A little. And I know the Head is concerned about the situation. Would you like to see her in the morning? I'll make an appointment for you, if you like. When are you free?'

'Second lesson.'

'Ten o'clock it will be then,' said Karen, writing in an appointment book. 'And if you don't come I'll send for you.'

'Thanks,' said Kate.

The walk down the hill from the school to the village in the cool, slightly dampish evening air restored Kate's health and spirits a little. She felt better, she decided, for having brought things to a head between herself and Celia. Hers was a temperament which didn't thrive on bottling up feelings. She had to show how she felt.

There were letters waiting for her at the flat, one from her grandmother and another in a long cream envelope, the address typewritten and in the left-hand corner the embossed name and address of the firm of lawyers to which Paul Holgate belonged. Kate's hands shook a little as she opened the cream envelope and her heart doubled its beat. At last she would know whether there had been any answer from Sean concerning a divorce. Quickly she pulled out the letter and scanned it, and the information it contained caused her heart to beat even faster.

'We have now heard from Mr Kierly. It seems that he is not willing at this time to agree to a divorce by mutual consent. He regrets the delay in answering our letter, but he did not receive it until recently. He is at present in the Middle East on an assignment.

Do you wish us to go ahead and file divorce proceedings against him? You have sufficient grounds to sue for divorce. Perhaps you will come up to our offices to discuss the matter at your earliest convenience.'

Slowly Kate folded the letter and placed it in the envelope. Now she knew why she hadn't heard from Sean. He had put his career before her as always. But why hadn't he agreed to a divorce by consent? What was the point in them staying married to each other when they didn't communicate and were never together? And what should she do now?

Oh, she was tired of worrying about it. If only she could

see him again, discuss the matter with him instead of with
Paul Holgate. If only she had stayed longer at Moyvalla. If
only she hadn't put her career first and hadn't rushed back
for an interview which had, after all, been nothing but a
farce. She had no one else to blame for the situation she was
in but herself and her own impulsiveness.

Next morning, promptly at ten she knocked on the door
of Miss Forbes office and was told to come in.

'Good morning, Miss Lawson. Please sit down,' said the
headmistress in her pleasant way.

The room was like a tranquil haven. Furnished with
elegant antique furniture, its apricot-coloured walls hung
with glowing original watercolours, its two long windows
draped in soft green velvet, it was designed to make anyone
who called to see the headmistress feel comfortable. Behind
the wide desk of carved oak Miss Forbes sat looking like a
benevolent lioness with her masses of tawny blonde hair
and heavily jowled face.

'Now what is the problem?' she asked, her dark grey eyes
flicking quickly over Kate's face.

Kate squared her shoulders and lifted her chin.

'I have to tell you that I find it impossible to work any
longer with Miss Fromsett,' she said, 'and I would like to
tender my resignation.'

The dark grey eyes blinked once, but the fair leonine
face remained impassive.

'I've been aware, of course, that you and she don't get on
very well,' Miss Forbes said at last slowly, 'but I was sure
that in time you would adjust to each other and learn to
work together to the benefit of the school community. May
I know in what areas there's friction between you?'

'We see everything from a different standpoint. She's a
strict disciplinarian and I'm not. She believes in imposing
discipline whereas I believe in encouraging self-discipline.

She says I'm not exact enough and several times she has interrupted private lessons to criticise me in front of my pupils. Last night the pupil was Carol Wyman, and she told the girl that she wasn't musical and shouldn't be taking music.'

Again Miss Forbes' face didn't alter, but she folded her thick-fingered white hands together on the desk in front of her and leaned forward slightly.

'You've done well with Carol,' she said. 'We've all noticed how much her behaviour has improved since you came to the school. In fact you've done well with all your pupils, and if you leave they'll miss you.' Miss Forbes paused, looked down at her hands, then looked up again, her eyes sharp and assessing. 'I've been expecting your resignation, ever since the first day of term, but not for the reason you have given just now.'

'Expecting it?' Kate was bewildered.

'That's right.'

'Why? Oh, surely you didn't think I would resign because I was disappointed not to be made head of the Music Department?'

'No. I thought you would be handing in your resignation because you're going to be married soon,' replied Miss Forbes, looking very severe. 'I have it on good authority that your future husband does not want you to continue to teach at Netherfield once you're married, and it was on the basis of that information that the interviewing committee decided not to award the position to you.'

'What good authority?' whispered Kate through dry lips.

'One of the members of the board of trustees supplied the information,' said Miss Forbes coldly. 'And it was felt it would be a waste of time to appoint you since you would be leaving the school so soon.'

'Then why was I interviewed?' demanded Kate.

'Attempts were made to tell you not to attend for the interview, but unfortunately they failed because you were away at the time, in Ireland, and there was no way we could contact you before the day.'

'So that's why the interview was so strange, and I was right, it was nothing more than a formality,' murmured Kate. 'Oh, I wish I'd known! I wish I'd known. I wouldn't have rushed back for it.' She realised Miss Forbes was staring at her in puzzlement. 'I only came to the interview because I believed I had a good chance of being appointed for the position since you'd suggested I apply for it,' she explained.

A faint flush of embarrassment crept across the head-mistress's normally pale face.

'I have to admit I encouraged you,' she said with a sigh. 'I would have liked to see you take on the challenge of organising the department and I was convinced you would do an admirable job. I was sure too that the interviewing committee would follow my wishes—but the conservatism of Colonel Critchelow won the day.' She smiled with a touch of cynicism. 'Since the majority of the committee have a financial interest in the school they had the last word and there was nothing I could do to persuade them that you would be more suitable for the job than Miss Fromsett. Do you understand?'

'I understand,' said Kate dully, and rose to her feet. 'I'll let you have my letter of resignation as soon as I've written it.'

'You realise, I hope, that it won't be possible to release you from your contract to teach here until Easter,' said Miss Forbes sharply, also standing up. 'And by then it's possible that you and Miss Fromsett might have resolved your differences.' Her face softening she came round the desk to stand before Kate. 'Don't be too hasty, please. It will be difficult to replace you at Easter. Let me speak to Miss Fromsett. In the interests of the school you and she should learn to work together.'

'I've done all I can to fit in with her ideas,' said Kate. 'And I don't think I can stay on and work with her knowing how she regards me. I'm sorry, but I'll have to resign. Thank you for telling me so much. You've been a great help. I know what to do now.'

Somehow Kate managed to get through the rest of the day without coming face to face with Celia Fromsett. School finished early because it was Friday and at three o'clock she left with a feeling of relief, the first time she had been glad that lessons were over for the week. The weather was still mild and moist, the sunshine filtering through a cloudy haze. Outside the house where she had her flat Barry's blue Mercedes sports was parked under the drooping branches of one of the huge chestnut trees, now bare of leaves. As soon as he saw her he got out of the car and came towards her.

'I couldn't get through another week without seeing you,' he said. His thin face was taut. There were dark smudges beneath his eyes and a muscle ticked at his jaw. 'How are you?'

'Quite well, thank you,' she replied automatically. She felt no excitement on seeing him. Nothing about him made her pulse leap. He was just Carol's father, whom she would rather not see just now, because she wanted to be by herself to think about Sean and herself, to plan what to do next. 'Barry, something unpleasant happened at school yesterday. It involved my lessons with Carol. . . .'

'I know. Carol phoned last night and told me. Kate, we must talk . . . about us. This waiting is beginning to get to me. I'm becoming a nervous wreck. I thought you might like to come riding and then go back to Rosedene for dinner, just the two of us . . . alone. Mother is away for the weekend.'

'I . . . I'll come riding, but I won't stay for dinner,' Kate said coolly, 'because I agree with you, we have to talk. I'll go and change.'

Three-quarters of an hour later, wearing a pair of faded jodhpurs and a thick yellow high-necked sweater, Kate sat astride one of Barry's hunters, a beautiful roan mare called Spitfire. Riding ahead of Barry, who was riding a powerful black gelding, she followed a path which crisscrossed the hill behind Rosedene.

Windless and mild, it was a perfect day for riding. Leather saddles creaked, harness jingled, hoofs made soft, slithering sounds on wet grass. Up and up they rode to a circle of tall grey-trunked beech trees, marking the site of an old Iron Age hill fort which had once been excavated but was now only a series of grass-covered mounds encircling a hollow filled with dying brown bracken and heaps of golden beech leaves.

Reining in, Kate waited for Barry to catch up. From this outlook she could see down a wide valley, patched with yellow and brown fields, each one edged by the dark smudges of hedges. A river made a shining silvery thread winding in wide loops, overhung by willows. In the distance the pointed steeple of a church glinted above a huddle of sloping house roofs.

'On a clear day you can see seven counties from here,' said Barry, as he reined in beside her. Both horses snorted and tossed their heads as they acknowledged each other. 'But not today. It's too misty.' He turned his horse so that he was facing her. 'Why won't you come back for dinner this evening?'

'Because I don't want to give anyone food for gossip

about me,' she replied steadily. 'Yesterday Celia Fromsett suggested I teach Carol the piano only because I want to please you. She accused me of being your mistress.'

'I wish to God she was right. I wish you were my mistress,' he said fiercely. 'Have you had any news about your divorce yet? Have you heard from Holgate?'

'Yes, I have. Yesterday. Sean has refused to agree to a divorce.'

Barry's face flushed a dull red, and since he was without a hat she saw the veins thicken on his forehead.

'Why? In heaven's name, why?' he demanded, almost choking on the words.

'I don't know.'

'So what are you going to do now?'

'Paul suggests that I go up to London and discuss the matter with him. He says I can sue for a divorce. I have sufficient grounds, but I . . .' She broke off, looking away from him, down at the silvery river, biting her lip as she felt sickness rising within her, the same sickness she had felt the day before when she had had the confrontation with Celia Fromsett. She swallowed hard and looked at Barry again, curiously. His tense attitude, the way his eyes were burning in their sockets was frightening. He seemed like a man on the verge of a nervous collapse. 'Barry, have you ever told anyone that I have agreed to marry you?' she asked.

The question surprised him. His fine blond eyebrows arched above his eyes and he blinked rapidly several times.

'I've told my mother that I hope to marry you one day,' he said slowly and rather cautiously, she thought. 'And I believe I have mentioned the matter to Carol . . . because I thought she would like it.'

'Anyone else?'

'Why do you ask?'

'This morning Miss Forbes told me why I didn't get the

job of head of the Music Department. She said it was because the interviewing committee had it on good authority that I was going to be married soon and that my future husband didn't want me to continue to teach at Netherfield, so they decided it would be foolish to appoint me.' Kate drew a deep breath and looked him challengingly in the eyes. 'You had no right to interfere in my life like that,' she added, 'no right at all. You did it deliberately, didn't you?'

For a few moments she thought he was going to lie and deny that he had used his position on the board of trustees to influence the interviewing committee. Tensely they stared at each other while the horses fidgeted restlessly.

'All right, I admit it,' Barry said at last. 'I did it because I'm damned if I'm going to share you with a career once we're married.'

'But we're not going to be married!'

'But you said . . .'

'I said I couldn't marry you because I'm married already and you agreed to withdraw your proposal until such time as I'd be free to give you an answer. Yet you went ahead and assumed I'd marry once I'd divorced Sean. You assumed too much, Barry. Even if I do divorce Sean I'm not going to marry you, not now.'

'You don't mean that,' he said, urging the black horse closer to the roan so that he was directly beside her, facing the opposite way. His face was taut and pale, the muscle at the jaw ticking wildly now. 'Miss Forbes shouldn't have told you about the deliberations of the interviewing committee,' he went on, and she could see he was speaking through set teeth. 'You're upset and . . .'

'Yes, I am, very upset. But I'm glad she told me, glad this has happened. I can see now what being married to you would be like—I'd never be able to call my soul my own,' she cried. 'At least . . .' Her throat clogged up and she had to swallow. 'At least,' she went on more steadily, 'at least Sean understood how I felt about the interview, and he didn't interfere or prevent me from leaving Ireland once he knew about it.'

Barry's eyes glared and his lips drew back over his teeth in a vicious grimace.

'So you've seen him,' he hissed. 'You saw him when you were in Ireland. But you didn't tell me.'

'Why should I tell you?' she flared. 'Why should I tell you anything about myself? Yes, I saw Sean.' She paused and on sudden impulse tossed caution aside. 'I saw him and I stayed with him and now . . . now I think I'm going to have his child.'

Violence glittered warningly in Barry's eyes and once again an ugly dark colour suffused his face.

'You bitch! You two-timing little bitch! You're no better than the rest after all,' he rasped.

His arm went up. Kate felt something sting her cheek sharply and realised with a sense of horror that he had hit her with his crop. His arm was going up again. Desperately she kneed her horse, lifting the reins to urge it forward, and the roan responded at once, plunging with a slither of hoofs down the steep slope. Once on the path she let the horse have its head. Excited by the freedom, it galloped swiftly and it was some time before she realised she was going in the wrong direction.

She looked behind her. Barry was following her and seemed to be shouting to her. She looked ahead and her mouth went dry. A few yards in front the path ended seemingly in mid-air. Frantically Kate pulled on the reins and ordered the horse to stop. Hoofs scrabbling on the stony surface of the path, it pulled up short on the brink of a disused quarry. Kate was jolted out of the saddle and over the horse's head. She fell with a sickening thud, banging her bare head on a protruding rock. She blacked out immediately, her fingers slid uselessly from the reins they had been clutching, and she rolled over and over down the incline to lie face downwards in a pool of brackish water that had collected in the bottom of the quarry.

She came round as she was being lifted on to a stretcher. Above she saw the sky clouding over and felt raindrops on her face. Someone was moaning. A face appeared, strangely slanted and poised above her. Something jabbed in her arm and the pain she could feel in the region of her pelvis receded deliciously. Once again darkness took over.

Later, much later, in a hospital ward she looked up to see another face, smooth-skinned with a faint golden tan.

'Sister Monica?' she croaked weakly, and looked round in a panic. 'Am I in the Mission hospital again?'

The face under dark curly hair topped by a white cap turned towards her. Small white teeth glinted and hazel eyes twinkled merrily.

'The name is Davies and I'm not a Sister yet, only a student nurse. And this is the General Hospital, not a Mission hospital. You're just coming round after the anaesthetic, so it's no wonder you're a little mixed up.'

'I fell, didn't I?' said Kate, relief flooding through her with the knowledge that she wasn't at the Santa Rosa Mission. 'Did I break anything?'

'No. You were lucky—nothing broken. Just a lot of bruises and some cracks. Oh, and a bang on the back of the head. But the doctor will tell you all about it next time she's round.'

The nurse went away. Kate closed her eyes and slept. She was wakened by another brisk nurse who came in early the next morning to check on her and help her to wash. Later the doctor came. She was a small Indian woman who wore a sari under her long white coat. She surveyed Kate with gentle brown eyes, then said softly,

'You were severely shaken up by that fall and you suffered a miscarriage. Did you know you were three months pregnant, Miss Lawson?'

'I ... I'd guessed,' whispered Kate, and feeling tears well in her eyes she turned her face away. After a while she asked, 'How long will I have to stay in hospital?'

'Until we're quite sure you haven't suffered any further internal damage and you've recovered from shock,' said the doctor. 'A week, perhaps ten days. It depends on how you behave and what arrangements can be made for you at home. It will be a few weeks before you'll be able to go back to work.'

In the afternoon Miss Forbes arrived to see her, bringing a bunch of tawny-gold chrysanthemums and a box of chocolates.

'From the staff,' she announced. 'How do you feel?'

'Weak,' said Kate.

'Is there any relative you would like me to inform? I've just been told it won't be possible for you to return to school until after Christmas.'

'Could you please write to my uncle, Hugh O'Connor, and tell him what's happened? I'll give you his address.'

'I was very disturbed when Mr Wyman phoned me to tell me what had happened to you,' Miss Forbes went on. 'He's coming to visit you this evening.'

'I don't want to see him,' said Kate, suddenly stubborn. 'Miss Forbes, please will you tell him not to come?'

'But the man is anxious about you. He seems to think it's his fault you have been hurt. He says he shouldn't have given you such a high-spirited horse to ride. You'll have to give him a chance to make an apology.'

Kate didn't argue any more. She was too tired and

weak. Miss Forbes left and the rest of the afternoon drifted by in a mist of desolation as Kate came to terms with the reality of the miscarriage and what it meant.

Evening visiting hours were from seven until nine and Barry walked down the ward at precisely seven o'clock, carrying a bouquet of hothouse roses. He looked quite normal, an urbane middle-aged businessman.

'I'm glad to hear you're all in one piece and that nothing was broken,' he said smoothly, taking the chair at the bedside. 'Whatever made you give the roan his head like that? I thought you had more knowledge of horses than that or I'd never have let you ride her.'

Kate stared at him in amazement, noting how smooth his face was, how empty his eyes. Was it possible he had forgotten his rage of the previous afternoon?

'I gave her her head to get away from you,' she said coldly. 'You were going to hit me again with your crop.' She touched her cheek with her fingertips.

'I hit you?' His eyes widened incredulously. 'My dear, I'd never do anything like that! You're imagining things. Possibly you're not right in the head—you certainly banged it hard. You should always wear a hat when you go riding, you know.'

'Please go away,' she said hoarsely. 'I don't want to see you again . . . ever.'

'Now I know you're not feeling right. I should have waited before coming to see you, but I felt very concerned about you.' Barry's glance roved over her shape, moulding the bedclothes, and came back to her face. 'Did you lose it?' he asked.

'Yes,' she whispered.

'I'm glad,' he said, triumph flickering in his eyes.

'Oh, go away, go away and never come back!' she cried, and turning her head on the pillow she closed her eyes.

Vaguely she heard the voice of one of the nurses speaking sharply, then Barry's voice answering with a touch of petulance followed by the sound of his footsteps retreating. He'd gone.

He didn't come to visit her again. Slowly Kate regained her strength and was able to leave the bed for several hours a day to sit in the lounge. In the evenings members of the school staff with whom she had been friendly visited her and on Saturday Hugh arrived. She told him everything.

'You little fool,' he remarked when she had finished. 'You proud, stubborn fool! And Sean's another proud fool for letting you leave him when you did. He should have insisted you stay with him at Moyvalla. Ah well, it's no use crying over it now. When are they going to let you out of this place?'

'The doctor said something about the day after tomorrow. But I won't be able to go back to work yet.'

'So you'll come back to Dublin with me and stay over Christmas until you're properly better. Gerry is just dying to mollycoddle you. You'll come?'

'Yes, please.' And for the first time since she had been hurt she let her tears flow freely.

Two weeks later, on a dark wet afternoon four days before Christmas, Kate sat at the piano in the parlour in Hugh's house and practised the music she was going to play at a Christmas concert to be held on Christmas Eve at the church Geraldine went to. Ever since she had arrived in Dublin, Hugh and Gerry had kept her busy, involving her completely in their way of life, never giving her a moment to brood over what had been or what might have been.

And they must be satisfied that their cure was working, she thought as she brought a carol to an end with a few quiet chords, because this afternoon they had left her in the house alone for the first time since she had come. They had gone to Dun Laoghaire to meet their son Gary, his wife Susan and their baby grandson Marcus off the ferry.

'I'd ask you to come with us,' Geraldine had said, 'but I'm expecting a parcel to be delivered this afternoon. Would you mind staying and taking it in for me?'

Kate looked at her watch. Four-thirty. Soon it would be dark and the parcel hadn't been delivered yet. She turned the page of the book of carols and had just lifted her hands to the keys when the front doorbell chimed.

She went through the shadowy hall and opened the front door. A man was standing there with his back to her, his white trenchcoat gleaming softly in the dusky light. He turned. She had an impression of a lean face tanned to the colour of teak, of grey eyes set under level dark eyebrows, of explosive energy kept under strict control.

For a surprised split second they stared at each other in silence, then the corner of Sean's mouth lifted in a slight smile.

'Hello, Kate,' he said. 'Is Hugh at home?'

CHAPTER NINE

STILL numbed by surprise, Kate continued to stare foolishly. Rain slanted down, drops beating a steady tattoo on the top step, soaking Sean's hair and streaming down his face. He raised a hand to wipe them away, his eyes narrowing, his eyebrows coming together in a frown.

'Are you all right?' he asked. 'Have you . . . have you lost your memory again? Don't you know who I am?'

'Oh . . . oh yes, I know who you are,' she croaked. 'I haven't lost my memory.'

'Thank God for that!' He looked relieved and then impatient. 'It's pretty wet standing out here,' he drawled dryly. 'Would you mind if I come into the house?'

'No . . . I mean yes. Come in. I'm sorry. You see I wasn't sure if . . .' Becoming aware that she was now babbling nervously, Kate stood back. Sean stepped past her into the hallway, pulled the door out of her hand and closed it. Then he turned to her and again there was silence as they stared at each other.

'You weren't sure if . . . what?' Sean prompted quietly.

'If I . . . if I . . .' Kate seemed to be very short of breath all of a sudden and her legs were beginning to shake. She had forgotten some things about him, she realised. She had forgotten that formidable explosive quality which had attracted her to him at their first meeting in San Marco. 'I wasn't sure if I was imagining it was you standing at the door,' she muttered, her eyelids fluttering down over her eyes as she avoided his bright observant gaze. 'Aunt Gerry asked me to stay in to take delivery of a parcel and I thought when the bell rang it would be the delivery man.'

'Sorry to disappoint you,' he drawled sardonically.

'Oh, I'm not disappointed,' she said hurriedly, looking at him again. 'Won't you take your coat off? Hugh and Gerry won't be long. They've gone to Dun Laoghaire to meet Gary and Susan and the baby off the ferry from Holyhead. Hang your coat over there and come into the kitchen. It's warm in there and I can make you some tea. I mean, would you like some tea?' She was babbling again, saying anything to try and make contact with him, to break through the proud shyness which seemed to build up around her whenever she met him.

'Tea would be fine,' he replied.

In the kitchen he sat on the couch while she filled the kettle and plugged it in. Now that the numbness had worn off Kate could feel excitement beating through her. He was here with her at last and anything could happen. Her hands shook as she took cups and saucers from the cupboard and the dishes rattled against each other.

'I heard you were on assignment in the Middle East,' she said. 'Have you just come from there?'

'By way of Westcourt and Netherfield School,' he replied coolly.

'Why . . . why did you go there?' she asked, trying to sound as cool as he did, trying not to show that she was again surprised as she set the cups and saucers on the table.

'Why do you think I went there?' he countered, and she gave him a quick wary glance. One of the cats had leapt up on to his knee and had settled there, and he was stroking it, not looking at her.

'Did you go to see me?' Kate quavered, and began to search another cupboard for Aunt Gerry's biscuit tin.

'I went there to see you,' he said mockingly. 'Why else would I go there? Fortunately the school secretary was still at the school and she was able to tell me you were here. She said you'd had to have time off at the end of term. She said you'd been ill. Are you better now?'

'Yes, thank you.' She began to arrange biscuits on a plate. 'I'm staying here until the school holidays are over.'

'When will that be?'

'Middle of January, about the fifteenth.' She put the plate of biscuits on the table and went back to unplug the kettle that was boiling.

'How did that interview go?' he asked. 'Did you get the promotion you wanted?'

'No.' She poured boiling water into the teapot. 'I was so sure I would get it,' she went on. 'I wouldn't have left . . . I mean, I would have stayed a little longer at Dunane if I'd been sure I would get the job.' She put the lid on the pot, covered with the knitted tea-cosy and carried it over to the table and sat down. 'Why did you go to see me?' she asked.

'For the same reason I was going to see you last Christmas but never made it,' Sean replied with a wry twist to his mouth. He pushed the cat from his knee, stood up and walked over to take a chair at the table and sit opposite to her. His narrowed glance flicked over her. 'You're too thin again,' he remarked softly. 'The secretary at the school said something about you having been thrown off a horse.'

'That's right,' she mumbled. 'But I'm all right now.'

There was silence for a few minutes, broken only by the pattering rain outside. Last Christmas Sean had wanted to see her to find out what she had done about dissolving their marriage. Now he was here for the same reason. Kate's spirits took a downward slide. The excitement faded, leaving her feeling dull and apathetic again. She looked across the table. Elbows resting on it, Sean was leaning slightly forward, folded hands in front of his mouth, watching her from under frowning eyebrows.

'I had a letter from your lawyer,' he said at last, slowly. 'It caught up with me in the Middle East. I wrote back refusing to agree to a divorce by consent.'

'I know,' she whispered. 'I had a letter from him telling me the day before . . . before I was thrown off the horse. I haven't been to see him yet to discuss what to do next. You see, I was so sure you would agree.' She looked at him again, trying to penetrate behind the handsome aquiline features and the cold clear grey eyes to what was in his mind and failing as usual. 'Why didn't you agree?' she asked.

His eyes were hidden by their lashes as his glance went to the plate of biscuits. Reaching out, he took one and bit into it, crunching it quickly between his teeth.

'I guess at the time of receiving the letter I didn't feel like agreeing,' he drawled lightly, and his eyes met hers again across the table, derision glinting in them. 'I never did like being pushed, you know, and often tend to do the opposite to what is suggested to me.'

'So if I . . . if I sue you for a divorce you'll fight it, I suppose,' she said rather sharply.

'I might. It'll depend on what you want to do after the divorce.'

'What do you mean?'

'I mean that if you intend to marry Wyman or any other man once you're divorced I won't let you divorce me.'

'But . . . oh, I don't understand you,' she blurted crossly. 'It was your idea in the first place. You suggested I do something about getting the marriage annulled when we were in Tuxtla and . . .'

'I know I did,' he cut in. 'But that was then, and at that time it seemed the right thing to do because I thought you shouldn't be held to the promises you'd made when you were suffering from amnesia. I thought you shouldn't feel . . . once you returned to England . . . that you were bound to me.' He reached out and took another biscuit. 'Am I ever going to get that tea?' he asked dryly.

Giving him an exasperated glance, Kate lifted the teapot and poured. Clear hot water came out of the spout. She stared at it incredulously and stopped pouring.

'Now look what you've done!' she accused, springing to her feet teapot in hand and glaring at him.

'I haven't done anything,' he retorted.

'You . . . you made me forget to put the tea-leaves in the pot!' she flared.

'I did?' His eyes widened and little glints of devilment began to dance in them. 'I had no idea I had such an effect on you.'

'Now you're being deliberately provocative,' she retorted haughtily, and turning away to the sink she poured the hot water away. 'And another thing . . . you never give a straight answer to a straight question,' she added as she plugged in the kettle again and reached for the tea-caddy.

'You're pretty good·at dodging issues yourself,' Sean jibed back nastily.

This time the silence was strained. Keeping her back to him, Kate stared out of the window. Darkness was thickening about the walls and chimneys of the houses and the back garden was wet and gloomy. She began to spoon tea-leaves into the pot.

'Wishing I hadn't come to see you?' Sean taunted, and she half turned to glare at him. Dark-haired and handsome, wearing a close-fitting high-necked sweater the colour of tobacco, he was a proud devil of a man with eyes that flared smokily with sulphur-coloured flecks.

'Yes,' she hissed between her teeth, saw his face go taut, his eyes harden icily, and changed her mind quickly, afraid suddenly that he would get up and walk out on her. 'I mean no. Oh, I don't know!' she wailed, and dropping the teaspoon full of tea into the teapot she covered her face with her hands, conflicting emotions tearing her apart. She had longed for Sean to come to her during the past months, yet now he was with her she found she was no nearer to knowing him. He was still a mystery, one she couldn't. fathom.

'I'm going to Moyvalla tomorrow,' he announced.

Dropping her hands from her face, Kate made the tea, forcing herself to be calm.

'Oh. Why?'

'At present it's the only home I have.'

'How long will you stay there?' She carried the teapot over to the table and sat down again.

'Until I go to Mexico. I've been appointed as manager of the agency's Central and South American news bureau in Mexico City, presumably because I speak Spanish and have experience of the region. I'll be based there more or less permanently for the next two or three years, depending on how I like it.' He gave her an underbrowed glance. 'You're welcome to come to Moyvalla with me, if you want to.'

She lifted the teapot and poured. This time the liquid came out in a golden-brown stream.

'I'm not sure,' she began hesitantly. 'If I did come, what would happen after Christmas and New Year are over?'

'You'd go back to your school, I guess. And I'd go to Mexico.'

'Then nothing would be changed.'

'What do you mean.'

'The situation . . . between us would be just the same as it has always been.'

'True. It will only change if you make it change.'

'But why should I be the one to make the change?' she argued. 'Why can't you?'

Sean didn't answer as he took the cup and saucer she had pushed towards him. Nor did he look at her.

'No,' she whispered as if speaking to herself, 'I can't do it. I can't go through it again. If we can't live together all the time we might as well not be married.'

While she poured tea for herself she gave him a surreptitious glance. He didn't seem disposed to argue with her. He didn't seem to care one way or the other what she did. He didn't care, that was it. Then why was he here?

The front door opened and then several voices echoed in the hallway, all talking at once.

'I take it you don't want to come to Moyvalla,' said Sean dryly.

'I can't come tomorrow,' she whispered.

'Okay. Forget it.' He shrugged his shoulders and finished drinking his tea.

'Sean, it's great to see you!' exclaimed Hugh as he strode into the room.

'Get some more cups out, Kate darling,' Geraldine ordered as she came in followed by Gary, Susan and the baby. 'And we'll all have a cup of that tea you've made. How long are you staying in Dublin, Sean? Over Christmas, I hope.'

'No. Just tonight,' Kate heard him answer as she took down cups and saucers.

'Then you'll stay with us,' said Geraldine firmly.

'You've got a houseful already,' he replied. 'I'll put up at one of the pubs in the city.'

'One more is neither here nor there,' argued Geraldine hospitably. 'Tell him, Hugh.'

'We can't have you staying in a hotel, not when Kate is here,' said Hugh. 'Besides, I want to hear all about the Middle East. I'm thinking of setting my next spy thriller out there. You'll stay the night and no argument,' he added. 'And I've some good malt whisky I'd like you to be testing.'

As she set out the cups and saucers Kate held her breath. If Sean refused to stay the night here she would know it was all over between them, she thought wildly.

'Okay, I'll stay,' he said, and she let her breath out.

'Of course you'll have to share a bed with Kate, but I'm sure you won't be minding that, now, will you?' said Hugh with a chuckle of ribald laughter as he twisted the cork out of a bottle of whisky and began to pour liquor into the glasses he had taken out.

'Kate and I have shared a bed before today,' Sean

replied smoothly, and across the table his glance challenged her.

'Would anyone like tea?' she asked, feeling her cheeks grow warm.

'Sure, Susan and I are just dying for a cup, aren't we?' said Geraldine. 'And then we'll go upstairs and put the baby to bed. Isn't he a darling, Kate? Just the spitting image of Gary when he was four months old.'

'I think he has a look of Susan about him,' argued Kate wickedly, and at once the age-old argument about which parent the baby most resembled began and she was able to ignore Sean.

Later, when Geraldine and Susan went upstairs, she went with them and into her bedroom. It wasn't long before Geraldine came in, her arms full of sheets and pillowcases.

'Aunt Gerry, couldn't you make up one of the beds in the attic for Sean?' Kate asked.

'And why should I be doing that when you and he are husband and wife and should be sleeping together, whenever you get the chance?' retorted Geraldine, whisking the cover and blankets off.

'I don't want to sleep with him. We ... I ... oh, we don't get on very well together. We're practically strangers and ...'

'I know how you're feeling,' said Geraldine, nodding her head. 'I used to feel the same when Hugh was a reporter and had been away for a long time. I used to feel I couldn't be bothered to adjust. But you'll get over it once you've been together a few days. You'll both be doing a little giving. That's all that's needed—a little giving. Or a little loving, if you prefer to put it that way. Come on now, help me put these clean sheets on.'

'But it's different from ... your situation with Uncle

Hugh,' muttered Kate as she smoothed a sheet. 'I mean, you and Hugh married because you loved each other and . . .'

'We married because we *thought* we loved each other,' interrupted Geraldine sharply, 'and found out only too quickly we didn't know a damn thing about loving. We had to learn it the hard way, and that's what marriage is all about, learning to love. It's a pity now that Sean can't stay longer than one night. Where's he off to tomorrow?'

'He's going to Moyvalla.'

'And there was me thinking he would be away to one of those foreign countries again. Then what's to stop you from going with him?'

'I can't go because I'm playing the piano for the children's carol concert. I can't let them down now. I was just telling Sean when you came in.'

'You won't be letting anyone down if you go with him. I can play for the concert instead. I would have been playing anyway if you hadn't been here. I only suggested you do it to help take your mind off that miscarriage.' Geraldine nodded and grinned as Kate gave her a sharp enquiring glance across the bed. 'Oh, yes, I know all about that. Hugh told me.'

'You won't tell Sean, please,' said Kate urgently. 'You're not to tell Sean about it, Aunt Gerry. I'll never speak to you again if you do!'

'No, I won't be telling Sean. I'll leave you to do that for yourself, as you should,' replied Geraldine. 'You are going to tell him, aren't you?' she added sharply.

'No.' Kate shook her head, pride in the tilt of her chin. 'I don't see why I should.'

'But it was . . . his child you lost!' exclaimed Geraldine. 'Or was it?'

'Of course it was!' snapped Kate.

'Then why not tell him?'

'Because I don't want him to think . . . oh, I suppose I don't want him to feel he has to be sorry for me.'

'My God!' breathed Geraldine. 'You've got the devil's own pride, like the rest of the O'Connors. And from what I've heard Hugh tell me about him, Sean is no better.' She turned towards the door. 'Don't you want to go to Moyvalla with him?'

'Yes, I do, but . . .'

'Then you'll tell him that you do, and you can forget about using the concert tomorrow as an excuse not to go.'

The evening passed pleasantly enough with the usual lively intellectual conversation Kate had come to expect in her uncle's house, but at ten-thirty, when it seemed that Sean and Gary were going to stay up all night talking and drinking whiskey with Hugh, Kate and Susan agreed they had had enough and after saying goodnight went up to their rooms.

Kate was determined to be asleep by the time Sean came but she was still wide awake when he entered the room. Pretending to be asleep, she kept her back turned to him and even when she felt the bed sink down under his weight she didn't move or speak.

The light went off and as soon as it did she was flooded with the bittersweet memory of their first night together in San Cristobal and her own innocent advances to him. And slowly the need to turn to him and speak to him became an ache gnawing away in the lower part of her stomach. Rigidly she lay, trying to control the passionage urges which were sweeping over her, gritting her teeth, clenching her hands, unaware that the sound of her breathing had changed, betraying the fact that she was not asleep.

'Kate?' His voice was soft and deep. 'Why don't you stop pretending? I know you're awake.'

She turned then, glad to release her limbs from rigidity. The darkness of the room was lightened by a glow from the street lamps coming through the window from which he had pulled back the curtains and she could see him, a dark shape against the light-reflecting whiteness of the pillow-slip.

He turned his head to look at her and she saw the glint of his eyes.

'Hugh has just told me what happened to you after that accident,' he said.

'Oh. I didn't want you to know,' she whispered miserably.

'Why not?' He sounded surprised. Then he asked with quiet bitterness, 'Because the child wasn't mine?'

'No, no. How could you think that?'

'You'd been friendly with Wyman.'

'But not that friendly,' she retorted tartly, and turned away from him again. 'I don't want to talk about it,' she mumbled.

Sean muttered an oath and putting his arm about her waist, dragged her back against him. Through her night-gown she could feel the warmth of him sweeping through to her and she longed suddenly to relax against him.

'You're damned well going to talk about it,' he whispered angrily, his arm tightening. 'We'll neither of us sleep a wink tonight if you don't. Why the hell did you go riding when you were pregnant?'

'I . . . I . . . didn't know I was. At least, I wasn't sure—I hadn't been to see a doctor. Anyway, riding itself wouldn't have done any damage and I wasn't expecting to be thrown off the horse.'

'Tell me what happened, Kate,' he asked more gently, and his hold on her relaxed a little, becoming subtly more dangerous because his fingers began to move slowly and seductively, inching upwards from her waist to her breast. 'I have to know for my own peace of mind, because if I hadn't insisted on sleeping with you that night at Dunane Castle you might not have become pregnant.' He paused and then she felt his lips move in a light caress on the side of her neck. 'I have a right to know,' he added, 'since it was my child you lost. Did the horse bolt with you?'

'Not really, but it was excited,' she replied. Closing her eyes, she recalled with a shudder that awful moment when she had seen the quarry yawning before her, a wide gulf waiting to swallow her up. 'I took the wrong direction,' she whispered, 'along a path to a deserted quarry. The horse stopped suddenly and I went over its head and knocked myself unconscious on a rock when I fell.'

'Was someone with you?'

'Yes.'

'Who?'

She didn't answer. She didn't want to think or remember any more, not when such delicious tingles were spreading along her nerves in response to the tender touch of his fingertips against her breast.

'Kate, I've got to know,' he whispered urgently, his breath warm against her cheek. 'Was Wyman with you?'

'Yes.' Her whispered answer was very thin, like a sigh in the light-dappled darkness.

His fingers were suddenly still, then his hand was withdrawn. He moved away from her on to his back and she felt cold and bereft.

'Did he know you were pregnant?' he asked. His voice was husky and it sounded as if he was having difficulty in controlling it.

'Not until I told him.'

'When did you tell him?'

'We had a quarrel,' she answered. 'While we were standing looking at the view from Banebury Circle. It's the ruins of an old Iron Age hill fort . . . like the one at Dunane Castle . . . built by the Ancient Britons. . . .'

'Okay, okay, forget that and get to the point,' he interrupted her sharply. 'Why did you and Wyman quarrel?'

'I'd found out that it was because of his interference I didn't get the job at Netherfield I'd hoped for.'

'How could he interfere with something like that?'

'He's a member of the board of trustees. He endows the school with money and he told members of the board who were on the interviewing committee that I was going to marry him and that he didn't want me to work at the school once I was his wife. So they voted against me, thinking it would be foolish to appoint someone who would be leaving the school soon. I was furious when I found out and I told him I was. And he . . . well, he hit me with his crop.'

The springs in the bed creaked as Sean reared up to lean over her, a dark shadow looming against the glow of light coming through the window.

'Did I hear that right?' he whispered. 'Did you say he hit you with his crop?'

'Yes, when I told him that I wasn't going to marry him even if I divorced you I let it slip out that I'd seen you in the summer and that I believed I was going to have your child.' Her voice shook. 'He was going to hit me again, so I urged the horse forward to get away from him.'

'You could have been killed!' Sean's voice cracked strangely and he began to revile Barry, calling him every unpleasant word he could think of.

'It was my fault,' Kate said urgently, sitting up beside him. 'I shouldn't have gone riding with him. And when I found out what he'd done deliberately to interfere with my career I lost my temper. I . . . I hadn't realised how unbalanced he was or how something like that could tip him over the edge into a sort of madness.'

'Have you seen him since?'

'He visited me in hospital. He . . . he said he was glad I'd miscarried.'

'I bet he was,' Sean muttered in a low fierce voice. He muttered a searing expletive and she saw his head go down on his bent knees, heard the long dragging breaths he was taking to assert control over himself.

'Sean.' Under her hand the skin of his bare shoulder felt like taut, stretched silk. He moved immediately, jerking away from her, sliding to the edge of the bed and swinging off it. 'Where are you going?' she exclaimed, peering through the darkness to see where he was.

'Downstairs.' The doorknob rattled as he turned it. 'After what you've been through recently you won't want to . . .' He broke off and she heard his breath hiss. 'You'll have a better night's rest without me being around. Goodnight.'

The door closed quietly and feeling the chilly night air stroke through her nightgown, Kate lay down again, hunching the bedclothes up about her chin and nose, missing Sean's warmth beside her, wishing contrarily that he hadn't gone, then wondering why he had.

A little giving, a little loving—Aunt Gerry's advice sang through her mind like a lullaby. Was that what Sean was doing by leaving her alone tonight, by holding his own needs under that tight control of his? Or had something else made him withdraw? Had the knowledge that she had lost his child turned him off?

Somehow talking with him had made her feel better. She felt purged suddenly of all anxiety and guilt and slid into the depths of sleep quickly. When she wakened at first light she could hear the baby crying in the next room and lay for a while watching light spread through the room, thinking of her cousin Gary and his wife Susan, their obvious happiness in being married to each other, their mutual delight in their baby. How had they attained that comfortable relationship with each other? Because they lived together. Because they had had the opportunity to learn about each other and to grow closer. She and Sean had never had that sort of opportunity. They hadn't had a chance to court each other, in the old-fashioned way, but had been plunged by circumstances into close contact without any sort of preparation.

And today, if she didn't do something, he would go away again and the chance to get to know each other better would be lost again. Clearly she saw now what she should do. Eagerness in all her movements, she left the bed, put on her dressing gown, thrust her feet into slippers and went down to the kitchen.

As she had expected Sean was on the chesterfield, hunched under the blanket which usually covered the back of it. He was apparently fast asleep with one cat sitting on his feet, the other stretched out beside him. Kate shooed the animals away and sat down on the edge of the couch, remembering the last time she had sat by him like this in the turret room at Dunane Castle and had wished she hadn't had to leave him.

Reaching out, she stroked the hair back from his brow and leaning forward pressed her lips to the smooth bareness of his shoulder from which the blanket had slipped down. He stiffened and she raised her head to smile at him. He didn't smile back but stared at her with wary sleep-hazed eyes.

'What do you want?' he drawled.

'To come to Moyvalla with you,' she replied. 'That is . . . if the invitation is still open.'

'And afterwards?' he queried, his eyes sharpening and narrowing.

'I'll have to go back to Netherfield. My resignation doesn't take effect until Easter,' she told him, looking at his mouth, admiring the long slightly crooked line of the upper lip and the stubborn, sensual thrust of the lower lip, wishing he would smile.

'You've resigned?' His eyebrow went up. 'Why?'

'I don't get on very well with the new head of the department,' she admitted, letting her hand stray with apparent casualness to his shoulder, her finger tips tracing the clean line of his collarbone that gleamed whitely through the suntanned skin. Against the back of her hand the tough bristles of his beard scratched as she caressed his jaw. Raising a hand, he took hold of her wrist, pulling her hand away from his face. But he didn't let go of her hand.

'What are you going to do? Have you found another position in another school?' he asked and though his voice was cool his eyes were not. The little flecks were flaring like yellow flames, mesmerising her.

'No. Not yet. I was thinking ...' She broke off and looked down. How to tell him? How to declare her love for him again in a way that he would believe? Their hands, seemingly beyond their control, were twining together, fingers interlocking, thumbs moving over skin in subtle caresses. 'I was wondering if at Easter ... I could join you in ... in Mexico, or wherever you might be,' she whispered.

His hand became still, gripping hers. Then he lifted hers and brushed his lips across the back of it. Kate looked up, her heart leaping. Above their joined hands Sean's eyes mocked her.

'You're thinking a long time ahead,' he drawled. 'But I'm sure something can be arranged to that effect. We'll talk about it at Moyvalla. With a bit of luck and fine weather we should be there by sunset.'

He was right. The sun was going down, shedding a long shimmer of golden light across a calm violet sea, when they stopped outside the old house. The front door opened at once and Agnes appeared. From behind her the Irish setter leapt, fully grown now. Plume-like tail waving ecstatically, it jumped up on Sean and she could see he was pleased because the dog remembered him.

'Sure and I had no idea you were coming, Miss Lawson,' Agnes grumbled, looking severely at Sean when they were all in the house, obviously displeased with him for not warning her about a guest.

'Mrs Kierly,' Sean corrected her, returning her disapproving glare blandly. 'It's time you knew. Kate is my wife.'

'You're married?' Agnes looked shocked. 'Well, I never! And there was me thinking that you and . . .' She broke off, shaking her head from side to side. 'Miss Cavanagh is going to be upset when she hears. She was over yesterday wanting to know if I'd heard from you. I told her I was expecting you today and she said she'll call again tomorrow.'

'Thanks for the message,' Sean said coldly, making for the stairs with his own and Kate's case. 'Is supper ready?'

'Sure it is. I'll just go and lay another place at the table,' replied Agnes huffily, and went down the hallway muttering, 'Married—well, I never!'

Slowly Kate made her way upstairs to the bathroom. As she washed her hands she stared at her reflection in the mirrow above the basin. She had forgotten about Nuala. Had Sean known the woman would be at Dunane for Christmas? Was that why he had wanted to come to Moyvalla? She would have to ask him outright. She had to know before she could rid herself of this awful suspicious jealousy.

Agnes didn't leave until after she had washed up and the kitchen was clean and tidy. Soon afterwards Sean went out with the dog. Alone in the bedroom Kate unpacked their cases and put their clothing away. Then she took a bath and changed into a long woollen lounging robe, dark Prussian blue figured with a paisley pattern in greens and reds, a perfect foil for her pale skin and glowing red hair.

She was sitting curled up on the couch, trying to read a book, wondering why Sean was out so long; wondering if, in fact, he had gone in the car to Dunane Castle, when he came in, the dog at his heels.

'Like some brandy?' he asked.

'Yes, please.'

He came over with two goblets and sat down beside her on the couch.

'*Slainte*,' he said.

'Happy Christmas,' Kate replied. 'At least I hope it will be happier for you than last Christmas was. I hope it will be happier for me too,' she added in a whisper, staring down into the tawny depths of the brandy. 'Sean . . . have you come here because you knew Nuala would be at the castle? Have you come tbe where she is?'

He set his glass down on the coffee table and turned to look at her.

'Why would I want to see her?' he said coolly.

'You went to Dublin to see her last Christmas. You went to see her before going to see me,' she muttered.

'I didn't go to Dublin with any deliberate plan to see her. I met her by chance in O'Connell Street and was foolish enough to go to that party with her.' His voice grated bitterly. 'I was foolish enough, too, to take her back to her apartment and tell her about you. She offered me a cup of coffee, to help me keep awake on the drive to Dun Laoghaire, she said. I accepted it because I trusted her. We'd been friends for a long time—that was why it was a while before I could bring myself to believe she'd put something in the coffee.'

'Something?' Eyes wide, Kate stared at him.

'Dope of some sort.' He leaned back, stretching his legs before him and stared at the fire.

'But why would she do something like that?' Kate whispered, horrified.

'She hoped I would pass out, there and then, at her place, so I'd miss the ferry and not be able to go and see you. She was hoping to seduce me while I was there. But I managed to leave, when I realised what she was after, and whatever she put in the coffee didn't have any effect on me until I was driving.' His mouth twisted sardonically. 'That's why I crashed. I was dozing while I was driving and the car lurched across the road into the path of the lorry.'

'Are you sure Nuala did that?' she asked, still horrified.

'I'm sure now. But at first I was just puzzled by the whole incident. You see, she was the first to come and see me in hospital and was very concerned about what had happened—too concerned, really. I asked her to write and tell you to come and visit me.' He sighed and turned his head to look at her. 'It wasn't until you came here last August and said you hadn't heard anything about the accident that I realised she hadn't written to you. After the banquet and the pageant were over at the castle I confronted her with the truth, and I could tell by the way she edged and blustered that I was right in my suspicions.'

'But why? Why?' demanded Kate.

'She was jealous of my rather fragile relationship with you,' he replied.

'But . . . you could have been killed in that accident!'

'That wasn't part of her plan, and I believe she was shaken up when she realised what she had done and possibly that's why she hovered around me all last summer like a broody hen. She was still determined to destroy our relationship, though, and did her best to turn you against me. The arrangement she talked about existed only in her imagination. I haven't had any arrangement with her or any other woman but you. You're the only one I've ever made any promises to.'

Kate sipped some brandy and put the glass down next to his on the table.

'You could have written to me yourself once you were better and convalescing,' she said.

'I did write, several times, but I tore up all my efforts,' he replied dryly.

'Oh. Why?'

'I told myself you wouldn't be interested in them. When you didn't come in answer to the letter I thought Nuala had sent to you I came to the conclusion that you'd ended the marriage and didn't want to know about me any more. It was what I'd expected you to do, so I decided the best thing I could do was put you out of my mind.' He laughed shortly. 'It was a lot harder to do than I'd believed,' he continued in a low bitter voice. 'Even when I drank too much I still thought about you. That was when I used to write to you. When I sobered up I destroyed what I'd written. I was in a pretty bad way when Hugh came to see me.'

'I know—he told me. That was why he tricked me into coming here.'

He turned to look at her again, his glance going over her slowly, feasting on her until she felt the blood pounding in her ears.

'Why are you looking at me like that?' she whispered.

'I can't help it,' he murmured, shifting towards her. 'When you turned up here last August I thought for a while I was seeing things. Then when you told me we were still married I went a little crazy and tried to keep you here so I could show you how much I loved and wanted you. It wasn't until you told me about that interview that I came to my senses and let you go.'

'Did ... did you say you ... you loved me?' she whispered incredulously. 'Just now?'

He reached out and touched her cheek, his fingers sliding across it to twist in her hair.

'That's right. I guess it happened when I first met you in San Marco, but it wasn't until you'd gone back to England that I realised what had happened to me. I used to think about you a lot and I made up my mind that if I ever got the chance to go to England I'd look you up.'

'But ... I don't understand,' Kate complained weakly.

'I was looking forward to seeing you again, last Christmas. I was hoping you'd done what I'd suggested and had dissolved the marriage so that when we met again we'd be free of its entanglement, free to find out if we loved each other enough to make a fresh commitment to marriage. But our meeting was delayed and when we met again you told me you didn't love me any more.'

'I believed I didn't, but while I was with you in August the feeling came back, stronger and deeper than before. I wanted to stay with you, but I was sure you wanted to be free of the marriage. Nuala had told me ...'

'To hell with Nuala!' he snarled. 'It was me you should have listened to, not her. Me you should have believed, not her. I hoped you'd got the message that night in the turret room at the castle, but it seems you didn't. You'd believe me now, if you really loved me. But I don't think you do.

You're in love with some image you've created, a sort of knight in shining armour who rescued you from the mission.' Bitterness rasped in his voice.

'No. That was true once, but not any more. I love you and want you—that's why I can't bear to be separated from you.' She saw his face stiffen, sensed his withdrawal, and leaned towards him urgently. 'I love you in every way I can think of. I do, I do,' she whispered desperately. 'Oh, what can I do to convince you that I'm not just being possessive? And how will I be able to endure being parted from you when I have to leave to go back to school and you go to Mexico?'

'You'll endure it because you'll know that I love you and will always love you, my dear, as it says in the old song "while the sands of life shall run",' Sean said softly. 'And because you'll know we're going to be together at Easter. That is if you'll come to me?' he added, lowering the banner of his pride at last and asking her.

'I'll come,' she promised, freed at last from her own pride. ' "I'll come to you again, my love," in the words of the same song, "Tho' t'were ten thousand mile." '

Her lips were ready for his kiss as he swept her against him.

'Let's go to bed,' he murmured thickly, his lips hot against the bareness of her throat, his fingers seeking seductively within the opening of her robe.

'Are you sure you want to share a bed with me? You didn't seem so keen last night,' she teased, ruffling his hair.

He lifted his head and she gasped with remorse at the tortured expression in his eyes.

'I was only teasing,' she whispered, her hand going up to his face to touch it consolingly.

'I left you last night because I couldn't stay and not make love to you,' he said huskily. 'I was afraid I might hurt you. It isn't long since you miscarried and ...' He broke off, pulling her against him, burying his face in the thickness of her hair. 'I could kill Wyman for what he did to you,' he muttered savagely.

'I'd no idea,' she said breathlessly. 'I'd no idea you felt like that about me.'

'This wild desire is something which gets beyond my control whenever I'm with you and whenever we share a bed,' he murmured, and pushed her away so he could look at her. Now he had his passion under control again. 'I'll sleep in another room if you like, Kate, until you're properly better,' he added coolly.

'I'm properly better now and I want to sleep with you, ache to be with you. I don't want to be apart from you longer than is necessary. I don't want to waste one moment of the time we'll have together here,' she whispered.

'Nor do I,' he replied, smiling at her at last. And taking her hand in his he pulled her up from the couch and together, arms about each other, they left the room and went upstairs.

DISCOVER...

SUPERROMANCE

From the publisher that understands how you feel about love.

Almost 400 pages of outstanding romance reading in every book!

Take these 4 best-selling novels FREE

Your **FREE** *gift includes*

Sweet Revenge by **Anne Mather**
Devil in a Silver Room by **Violet Winspear**
Gates of Steel by **Anne Hampson**
No Quarter Asked by **Janet Dailey**

FREE Gift Certificate
and subscription reservation

Mail this coupon today!

In the U.S.A.
1440 South Priest Drive
Tempe, AZ 85281

In Canada
649 Ontario Street
Stratford, Ontario N5A 6W2

Harlequin Reader Service:

Please send me my 4 Harlequin Presents books free. Also, reserve a subscription to the 6 new Harlequin Presents novels published each month. Each month I will receive 6 new Presents novels at the low price of $1.50 each [*Total - $9.00 per month*].. There are no shipping and handling or any other hidden charges. I am free to cancel at any time, but even if I do, these first 4 books are still mine to keep absolutely FREE without any obligation.

NAME   (PLEASE PRINT)

ADDRESS

CITY   STATE / PROV   ZIP / POSTAL CODE

Offer expires December 31, 1981
Offer not valid to present subscribers   BP434

Prices subject to change without notice.